THE SNOW ORPHAN'S DESTINY

DAISY CARTER

❀ Created with Vellum

CHAPTER 1

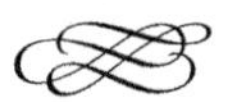

South Wales - 1846

THE YOUNG WOMAN pulled her threadbare cloak tighter around herself as she turned the corner into Caradog Street, drawing the hood lower over her brow to cover her hair. She had been walking for what felt like hours. Her feet were numb from the icy slush that seeped through the holes in her boots, but the thought of warmth and shelter propelled her forward.

"Mind yerself," the lamplighter shouted as he manoeuvred his ladder against the street light. Pools of dim orange light showed how far he had progressed along the street, and he whistled cheerily as he started climbing the wooden rungs. From his elevated position, he paused for a moment to watch the woman. She made a lonely figure amidst the general merriment of the town in the festive season, and there was something about the way she was walking that looked slightly strange. "Too much gin, no doubt," he muttered to himself, shaking his head. "Are you alright, miss?" he called after her. In a few hours, there would be plenty of drunks turning out from the taverns, and like most of the town's lamplighters, he took his other role as a nightwatchman seriously.

"Miss! I said, are you alright?" He scrambled back down his ladder, feeling exasperated that she had ignored him.

"Yes…I…I'm fine…nearly at my destination, thank you for asking." The woman seemed distracted as she glanced back over her shoulder at him.

"Well, don't dawdle. It ain't the sort of night for a woman to be out alone, and it's starting to snow again." The lamplighter hefted his ladder onto his shoulder again and strode onwards, his thoughts turning to the warm spiced ale that his wife had promised to make for when he got home.

The woman glanced back over her shoulder

again, wondering for a brief moment whether she should stay near the lamplighter instead of continuing on alone. His concern for her welfare felt like a soothing balm to her troubled soul. She could barely remember the last time anyone had noticed her, let alone asked if she was alright, and she fantasised about being welcomed to his humble home by a rosy-cheeked wife clucking over her as they took pity on her situation.

"No. It's not much further," she whispered to herself. Besides, she shouldn't need to rely on the kindness of strangers, not with her family name. She lifted her chin with renewed determination. She would continue with the plan which had slowly taken shape in her mind that morning when she had realised that it was Christmas eve. Since she had come to the decision, she had been buoyed up by a renewed sense of optimism, telling herself that surely they wouldn't turn her away today of all days. It was a time for forgiveness and good deeds, after all.

As she plodded through the snow-covered streets, the woman couldn't help but feel cheered by what she saw. The shop windows were decorated to entice shoppers in, with candles and colourful displays. Toffees and peppermint sticks jostled with brightly painted wooden toys in one. Embroidered handkerchiefs and jewel-like silk shawls were artfully arranged in the bow window of the dressmaker. Even the clockmaker and cobbler had ribbons of tinsel wound around sprigs of holly as they worked into the evening to fulfil their last few orders of the season before a precious couple of days off.

Most of the shopkeepers of Brynwell-On-Sea were open later than usual, hoping to make a few last-minute sales to the workers trudging home from the offices, factories, and docks with a few extra coins in their pockets from the employers who had been generous enough to give them a bonus.

"Hot coffee with a splash of rum for you?" A wizened old man beamed at her from his makeshift stall.

"Roasted chestnuts..." his neighbour cried, holding out a paper twist of the hot treats.

She shook her head. "No thank you."

Costermongers jostled and shouted in the market square as they fought to catch the attention of the maids who scurried past, running the last few errands for their mistresses before the weather took a turn for the worse. People had been talking about a possible snowstorm for days, and the wind was starting to pick up.

The woman's mouth watered as she paused to rest outside a bakery. The aroma of cinnamon and nutmeg wafted out, and she looked longingly at the display of rich shortcrust meat pies and sticky currant buns. The proprietor eyed her up and bustled out from behind the counter to stand in the doorway.

"I can do you a bag of yesterday's bread for a farthing," he said, looking at the sodden, ragged hem of her cloak. "It's a bit stale, but it'll fill you up."

The woman's head swam as she tried to concentrate on what he was saying, and her stomach cramped with hunger as she watched his wife carrying a tray of bread rolls, fresh out of the oven, to display next to the currant buns.

"Sorry, I don't have enough money," she whispered.

The baker's eyes narrowed. "Be on your way then. I don't want you blocking the window, you're putting the other folks off their shopping, hanging around like a beggar."

As the woman rounded the corner into Alba Street an hour later, the wind tugged at her cloak, and the snowflakes swirled, making her feel dizzy. She stumbled onwards, holding onto the ornate metal railings along the front of the houses to steady herself until, finally, she reached her destination. Parkhouse Villa.

A gasp of relief escaped from her lips as she clambered up the steps. The snow was settling fast, and it was hard to see where to place her feet, but she knew she had to take care. At the top of the steps, she gazed through the window into the opulent drawing room on her right. She could see a fire blazing in the hearth, and there was an extravagantly decorated Christmas tree next to the piano where a woman with blonde ringlets was playing. A maid was circulating between the guests, offering glasses of sherry or fruit punch on a silver platter as well as tiny morsels of fancy food that could be eaten in one mouthful. The master of the house, a tall gentleman with mutton-chop whiskers, was standing with his back to the fire, gesticulating as he came to the conclusion of a story that made everyone roar with laughter.

It was a scene that tugged at the woman's heartstrings, such was the comfort and familiarity of it from years gone by. She could see that everyone was in high spirits and her mouth curved into a soft smile to match the festive sentiment from inside.

"Safe at last," she murmured, raising her hand to lift the heavy brass knocker on the front door.

"WHAT ARE YOU DOING HERE?" The man with the mutton-chop whiskers wasn't laughing anymore. "It's Christmas eve, and we're entertaining." His voice was hard and uncompromising as he stood in the doorway, glancing over his shoulder in case anyone else came out into the hall.

"I know," the woman said quietly, feeling sad that he wouldn't want her to be seen by his guests. "That's why I came. You're my last hope. Could you find it in your heart to—"

"Certainly not," he snapped, cutting her off. He glared at the maid who was hovering nearby. "You shouldn't have answered the door to this wretched creature," he said in a scolding tone that made the poor woman bob her head meekly. "I thought I'd made it clear that I don't want her sort in my home."

The maid twisted the corner of her apron and bobbed her head nervously again. "I'm sorry, Sir. I thought that, seeing as it's Christmas, you might make an exception. Per'aps we could give her a hot meal in the servant's quarters, Sir. There's a bit of stew left over. It wouldn't harm, would it, 'afore we send her on her way again."

The man's expression darkened. "I won't have this scandal brought to my doorstep. Think what it would do for my reputation. My clients rely on me to be an upstanding man of the community who they can trust."

"Please…" the young woman begged. She stepped forward and let her cloak fall open, hoping that if he understood the true extent of her plight, he might find a shred of pity in his heart and let her in. "Please, will you help me? I don't have anywhere else to go, and I promise you'll hardly even know I'm here. Just for a few weeks?" She reached out and rested her hand on his sleeve, but he recoiled in irritation, shaking her off.

"Begone with you," he whispered harshly, glancing back towards the sound of laughter coming from his drawing room again. "You're a disgrace, and if I see you loitering on this street, I'll have the constable throw you in jail for causing an affray."

The woman stumbled backwards as though she had been slapped, and a moment later, he slammed the heavy door in her face to underline his words. There was no welcome to be had from him.

She almost slipped as she picked her way back down the steps. It was getting harder to recognise the familiar landmarks of the town, and she hesitated for a moment before trudging back the way she had come. Not that it really mattered which direction she was heading in any longer. It made no difference; all that mattered was that she should find shelter for what was to come.

"Miss! Wait, Miss Louisa."

The woman spun around as she heard her name being called, and hope flared in her chest. It was the maid hurrying after her.

"Did he change his mind?"

"I'm sorry." The maid shook her head apologetically. "I tried to persuade him, but I daren't say too much in case I lose my job." She dug into her apron pocket and pulled something out. "Take this, miss. It's not much, but it's all I had on me, and it might help in a small way." She jumped nervously as the sound of raucous laughter from a nearby tavern filled the night air. "I'd best get back. The master will be expecting us to serve dinner in a minute, and if I'm covered in snow, he'll know I came out to see you." She lifted her skirts and hurried away. "God bless you, Miss Louisa...and good luck."

Louisa looked down at what the maid had pressed into her hand. It was one penny and her eyes suddenly filled with tears of gratitude at the kindhearted gesture. It would be enough to buy some hot food, which would see her through the night while she tried to think of what to do next.

"Thank you," she called after the maid's retreating back. If she hurried, she might even be able to get the stale bread that the baker had offered her as well, which would do her for several days.

The snow was falling even faster as Louisa retraced her steps along Alba Street. Not that she could see her footprints. They had long gone, obliterated by the new snow that was now so deep it dragged at the hem of her cloak, slowing her down. Every step was an effort, and she wondered if she had the energy to carry on.

Suddenly, Louisa became aware of someone behind her. The warm cheer from the men leaving the tavern seemed a long way away, and most of the clerks had already gone home. The street felt almost deserted, and she hastily tightened her old cotton scarf over the collar of her dress out of habit. What lay under the scarf was the only link to her past, and she knew a pickpocket would think nothing of stealing it from her.

"Are you lost? It's a mucky sort of night to be out alone." A tall figure loomed out of the shadows, and Louisa found herself looking up into the cold gaze of a burly man in a greatcoat. "Why don't you let me take care of you..." His hand snaked out, and he grabbed her arm, giving her a thin smile. "My lodgings are nearby. If you do as you're told, I might even give you a tot of rum for your troubles."

Louisa drew herself up to her full height, trying not to show her fear. "Let go of me. I'm just on my way home, and my husband is expecting me."

"Come now, don't take me for a fool," he scoffed. "I was outside the tavern, and I saw you being turned away from that toff's house on Alba Street. I reckon you could do with a roof over your head tonight, so you may as well give me what I want. Perhaps I'll even take you on as one of my ladies of the night. You're pretty enough." He pulled her hood down and pinched her cheek with a thoughtful expression.

"No...I'm not that sort of woman." Louisa wrenched her arm free, feeling a surge of strength out of desperation. "Leave me alone." She turned and ran as fast as she could, stumbling through the drifting snow until her breath came in ragged gasps. The winding streets narrowed, and she had no idea where she was. Just when it felt as though she couldn't go on for a moment longer, she saw a narrow alleyway between two tall buildings. The cobbles were mercifully free of snow where they had been protected by the leaning rooftops above, and she summoned the last of her energy to change direction, hoping that the man wasn't following. When she emerged at the other end, her heart lifted as she spotted a row of stables with a coach house over the top, and she thought longingly of the soft straw. If she could find a way in without anyone noticing, it would give her some sort of shelter from the snowstorm for the night, so she could rest. She kept her gaze fixed on the archway that led to the stables, not daring to look behind her and stepped out into the street. The sound of her own gasping breath filled her head, and she clutched her side as a wave of pain engulfed her.

"Lookout!" A shout of warning split the air just as a drayman's wagon rumbled past right in front of her.

Louisa staggered backwards on the icy cobbles, her arms flailing as she tried to stay upright. The last thing she remembered was the way the snowflakes seemed to dance in the air above her as she fell to the ground, and then darkness claimed her.

CHAPTER 2

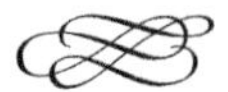

"Those oranges will do nicely for the little 'uns. You've got a good heart, Bernard." Maude Bevan smacked a hearty kiss on the cheek of her favourite costermonger, making the old man chuckle.

"I'm sure my wife would agree," he replied as he packed up his handcart to go home. "Enjoy yourselves tomorrow."

Maude waved as she hurried away, draping a cloth over the top of her basket to keep the snow off the last few items she had purchased for Christmas. Mr Culpepper, the manager of Culpepper's Brickworks, had let them finish work a couple of hours early in a rare display of generosity, although Maude suspected it was more to do with the fact that there were rumours of a new business partner joining soon. Usually, the old curmudgeon paid no heed to holidays, but perhaps he wanted to create the impression that he cared about his workers. At least until the deal was struck, she thought to herself.

"Merry Christmas to you and your family, Maude," the butcher called as she passed. "How are you and the children doing? It will be a difficult few days for you all, I expect."

"Work keeps our minds off it, but yes, it's a strange old time without my Fred. You know how much he loved this time of year."

Maude's progress through town was slow as she paused to chat with her friends and acquaintances. It helped fill the ache of missing her husband, who had died from pneumonia the previous winter. The illness had taken him a week before Christmas, which had made it even harder to bear, but she was determined to make the next few days jolly for the sake of her children. Nell and Jacob, her four-year-old twins, were as thick as thieves and had been too young to appreciate what happened. But Tom had taken it harder, being that bit older. She knew that he missed his pa's steady presence as much as she did. The evenings were the worst. Fred used to sit by the fire and read out snippets from the old newspapers he collected after the wealthy folk had finished with them or whittle wooden toys for the children. But now his armchair was empty, and she was struggling to make ends meet.

The snow was falling faster than ever as she left the shops behind and followed the familiar route home, weaving through the market traders and standing back to avoid getting sprayed with slush from the heavy wagons that rumbled past. Her thoughts turned to the festive day ahead, and it lifted her melancholy spirits. Fred would have wanted them to celebrate the same as usual, and she could already imagine the squeals of excitement from the twins in the morning when they discovered the stockings laden with treats by the hearth. It would make all the extra hours she had worked at Culpepper's Brickworks since the summer worthwhile to see their happy smiles.

"Give me some room." A thickset drayman scowled at Maude as she edged past him in the darkness. "Honestly, I don't know what the world's coming to these days," he continued. "Folk don't look where they're going. It ain't as if my wagon is hard to miss."

"Sorry, I was distracted by all the twinkling candles in everyone's windows. They look lovely and festive, don't you think?" She gave him a warm smile, hoping to lift his mood.

"Don't people realise I've got a family to get home to as well?" he harrumphed as if Maude was to blame for him still being out working. "That silly woman stepped right out in front of me just now. If I hadn't been paying attention, my horses could have taken fright and bolted." He grunted with exertion as he lifted one of the oak barrels on his wagon onto his shoulder and headed towards The Saddlers Arms tavern. The sound of a tinkling piano and singing drifted from the doorway as two men stumbled out. "Lookout, gentlemen. This is my last delivery of ale for the day." The drayman sounded more cheerful at the thought of being paid and perhaps a nip of brandy to see him on his way.

Maude continued along Sketty Lane. She could see the mews up ahead where the horses for the wealthy family who lived in the big house beyond were stabled, which meant that her walk was almost over. Her own modest home, Willow Cottage, was one of eight identical houses around a small cobbled courtyard that lay a bit further along from the mews. It was a vast improvement on the draughty rooms in the old tenement building by the docks where she and Fred had lived when they first got married and was one of the reasons why Fred had taken up work for Mr Culpepper as his clerk because the cottage came with the job.

Suddenly her attention was caught by a muffled groan from the entrance to the alleyway opposite the mews. She strained her eyes in the gloom and saw a dark shape on the ground. At first glance, it looked like a mound of rags, but then she heard another groaning sound.

"Is this what the drayman was talking about?" she muttered, crossing over to take a closer look. She noticed that the snow was churned up in the road where the horses had presumably reared and swerved.

Maude fell to her knees. "Are you alright, dear?" In the weak lamplight, she could see that it was indeed a young woman. There was a spattering of scarlet blood on the snow next to her head, and the woman groaned again as her eyelids fluttered open.

"You've had an accident. I think you must have been knocked over by the dray wagon. Can you sit up?" Maude tutted at the realisation that the drayman hadn't even stopped to see how the woman was before looking around to see if someone could help her. The young woman felt like a dead weight in her arms as she tried to heave her upright.

The only person she could see was a tall man halfway down the alley. "You there…can you help me?" She beckoned him over.

The man lingered in the shadows for a moment and then came closer. There was something about his demeanour and the proprietorial way he was eying the woman that Maude didn't like, but she pushed her misgivings aside. "Do you know this young lady?" she asked.

"Never seen her before," the man said hastily. He darted a look up and down the street before reaching down to grasp her arm and pull her upright, so she was sitting against the wall.

"What's your name, dear? We'll take you home if you can tell us who you are." Maude pulled a handkerchief out of her apron and dabbed it gently on the cut on the woman's head. "You took a fall, but I think you'll be alright."

"I…I don't know," the woman replied. She blinked as though struggling to focus.

"I heard someone call her Louisa," the man ventured.

"What direction was she coming from? Did you see if she was with anyone else?" Maude peppered him with questions.

"I…have I seen you before?" the woman asked, peering upwards and trying to focus on the man's face. "You look familiar…but I can't quite remember. Weren't we talking, and then…I was running…"

"No, we've never met." The man stepped back into the shadows to distance himself from the situation. He shrugged as he looked back at Maude. "It's nothing to do with me. All I heard was her name, and she seemed to be in a tearing hurry. She should have looked where she was going; that's all I can say."

"Gently does it." Maude offered her arm as the woman struggled to her feet and then gasped as her voluminous cloak fell open. "You're with child, my dear. And not long to go, I should say. Are you sure you don't know her?" she asked the man again, giving him a suspicious look. "She seems to think she knows you."

"No," he said firmly, eying Louisa's swollen belly. "And I don't want anything to do with her either. I've got business to attend to, so I'll be on my way." With that, he lifted his hat and gave Maude a curt nod before hurrying away.

"So much for helping those in need. A fine sort of fellow you are," Maude called after him, her voice laced with annoyance.

"I'll be fine. I don't want to put you to any trouble." The woman swayed and then clutched her side. "If I keep walking, I'm sure I'll find somewhere to shelter soon. I think I was on my way to the stables, but it's all very hazy in my mind," she confessed, giving Maude a guilty smile.

"I know this is Christmas, but we don't need to recreate the nativity scene right here in Sketty Lane, my dear." Maude picked her basket up and took hold of Louisa's arm. "My cottage is just along the way. You'll come home with me, and I won't hear another word about it. It's not the grandest place, but you'll be warm and dry. I think that's the least we can do for the baby, don't you?"

"SHALL I show the lady my dolly, Ma?" Little Nell tugged on Maude's skirt and her eyes rounded with alarm at the muffled groan of pain that came from their new guest. "Is she sick like Pa was?"

"No, poppet," Maude said hastily. "She's not sick. I reckon it's the baby on its way. I got her back to the house just in time."

Jacob paused from where he had been coaxing the fire into life with the bellows. "Who is she, Ma?" His question was whispered because he had been taught it was rude to talk about other people, but his curiosity had got the better of him.

"Here, let me do that." Eight-year-old Tom nudged his younger brother aside and pumped the bellows with gusto, and a moment later, orange flames licked around the coal, and the room started to feel a bit warmer.

"Louisa is my name. Louisa...." The woman pressed her lips together in frustration. "My surname is on the tip of my tongue, but I can't quite remember it...or much else for that matter."

Maude gave her a reassuring smile. "I expect it will all come back to you once that bump on your head has gone down, dear. But until you remember your full name and where you live, you can stay here with us." She put the kettle on top of the range to boil and bustled to the linen cupboard to fetch some clean sheets.

"I'm so sorry you've had your Christmas eve ruined," Louisa said as she watched Maude. She looked helplessly down at the large bump under her gown. "If only I could remember...I expect my family must be wondering where I am."

"All in good time." Maude poured Louisa a cup of tea and put it on the table next to her, discreetly looking her over for clues as to who she might be. Louisa's hands were red and chapped as though she was used to physical labour, but the way she spoke and the fine features in her oval face seemed to imply that she came from a higher class background. Perhaps she had been widowed and fallen on hard times. Maude knew all too well how quickly a woman's circumstances could change.

"I'd like to give you something for taking care of me." Louisa cast her eye around the room. "Is my reticule here?"

"I'm afraid you didn't have anything with you, just the clothes you're wearing."

Louisa's face fell, and she looked embarrassed and confused. "Are you sure?" She shook her head slightly, willing the memories to return.

Before she could say anything more, a fresh wave of pain engulfed her, and she gave Maude a worried look when it eventually passed. "I'm not sure I feel ready for this. How can I become a mother if I don't even know who I am?" Her eyes filled with tears as she realised she was completely dependent on the goodwill of strangers.

"You're young, and you'll be surprised how different you'll feel once the baby arrives." Maude's eyes misted over as she remembered having Tom and how Fred had doted on their three children. "How are you feeling now?" she asked.

Louisa leaned back in the armchair and closed her eyes for a moment. Her head ached, but more worryingly, she realised the pain across her back and abdomen was deepening and seemed to be coming more regularly. She rubbed her hand over her belly and groaned as a fresh spasm gripped her.

"Tom, I'd like you to run along the street and fetch old Mrs Dyer." Maude kept her tone light, but a shadow of worry crossed her face. "Tell her we have a young lady staying with us who needs her help."

"Is she having the baby right now?" Tom pulled his hobnail boots on hastily. Ethel Dyer was the local midwife, which could mean only one thing.

"I think we might have a new arrival before the

night is out," Maude told her son with a quick nod. "Run along and tell her to hurry."

Tom sprinted out into the snowy night, and the twins showed Louisa their favourite toys as she drifted in and out of lucidness.

* * *

"It's a girl," Ethel Dyer announced an hour later as the house filled with the lusty wail of a newborn baby.

"Praise be!" Maude dabbed the tears of happiness from her eyes and looked down at the little mite once Ethel had deftly swaddled her in a soft, clean sheet. The baby looked up unblinkingly with wide, dark eyes, taking everything in. Aside from her first cries, she seemed remarkably content, and Maude sniffed again and blinked back fresh tears. "What a miracle that I found Louisa and we could get her safely inside."

"Don't speak too soon," Ethel said in a low voice. She brushed the matted hair from Louisa's forehead and frowned slightly. "She looks frail. I don't think she was in very good health to start with, and having such a quick birth has taken it out of her. It's a good thing you fetched me when you did."

"Well, she's in the best place now. We have plenty of food for Christmas, so I'm sure she'll get well again after a few days' rest."

Louisa's eyes fluttered open at the sound of the baby's whimpers, and her expression softened as soon as Ethel laid the baby on her chest.

"Hello, little one," she whispered.

"I'll make us all a nice cup of tea," said Maude. She could remember being parched with thirst after having Tom, and Louisa looked like she hadn't had any sustenance for a while.

"Ma...this fell out of Louisa's pocket." Tom was hovering outside the bedroom door, waiting for news, and he handed Maude a coin. "I saw it when you were helping her to bed."

"It's a penny." Maude nodded approvingly. Some boys might have been tempted to keep the money, but Fred had raised Tom, to be honest. "That's all she has to her name." She felt a pang of sadness for the young woman, wondering if someone might be missing her.

Suddenly Ethel called her back into the bedroom. "She's taken a turn for the worse, losing a lot of blood. We need to send for the doctor."

For the second time that night, Tom was dispatched to get help, and Doctor Willis returned not long after, accompanied by a blast of icy air as he let himself into the small cottage.

His expression was grave when he finally emerged from the bedroom. "I think you need to prepare yourself for bad news," he said as he wound his scarf back around his neck. "The girl is malnourished, and I think she might be suffering from the lingering effects of influenza, I'm afraid to say." He shook his head and sighed. "Another poor wretch who has found herself in desperate times."

"We can't even tell her family," said Maude. "She fell and bumped her head. All I know about her is that she's called Louisa if that man in the alley is to be believed."

"What about the baby? Was Louisa well enough to say what she wanted to call her child?" Doctor Willis glanced at the clock on the mantel shelf. It would soon be midnight, and no doubt there would be more patients to see before he managed to get to bed. "The snow has stopped, but there's a hard frost setting in now. I'll have to get on my way."

Maude shook her head. "She was barely lucid."

Her eye caught the coin which she had asked Tom to leave on the table for Louisa to have once she was well enough to get up again.

"Penny," she said softly. "We'll call the baby Penny...just until Louisa recovers."

CHAPTER 3

"Would you like some mistletoe to take home, Sir? Or perhaps a sprig of holly and ivy?" Penny gave the gentleman in the well-cut frock coat her most persuasive smile as he strolled past.

"Shall we, dear? I know we've already decorated the parlour, but we could always add more." The elegant woman on his arm paused, pulling her fur-trimmed cloak tighter against the cold wind.

"I know you like to support these street sellers, but where would we put it during the show?" The man looked snootily down his nose at Penny and then glanced in the direction of the theatre.

"I could look after it until you come back out of the theatre," Penny said hastily. Although she was only coming up for eight years old, she knew how to charm the toffs and tell them what they wanted to hear. "It was freshly cut this morning, Miss. I'm sure it will go a treat in your parlour."

She could see the gentleman weakening, wanting to please his wife. "I'll even tie some red velvet ribbon around it. I only do that for my best customers," she added, giving them a little curtsey. "I'd be ever so grateful…my ma's not well, you see, and every farthing counts in this terrible weather when there are so many of us at home to feed."

"How can we resist such a sweet little girl, Geoffrey?" The woman gave her husband a doting smile, and he handed Penny a couple of coins.

"I'll take the mistletoe now and ask the manager at the theatre to look after it for us," he said, giving Penny a stern look. "I know what you lot are like. You'll be off with my money as soon as our backs are turned. I wouldn't have bothered if it weren't to please my dear wife. She has a rather quaint notion that we should support the endeavours of the poor, whereas I believe you'd be better off working in one of the factories instead of loitering on the streets like this."

Penny meekly handed the mistletoe to him and pocketed the coins. She wanted to tell the man that she had been standing for so long in the snow that she had lost the feeling in her toes hours ago and that her back was aching, just like it did every day, but she knew it would fall on deaf ears. Instead, she bobbed her head and gave them another ingratiating smile, this time looking directly at the woman. "Thank you, Miss…Sir…I appreciate your custom, and I hope you enjoy the play."

The woman nodded happily. "You see, Geoffrey, it feels nice to do our little bit to help the needy. Now, we'd better hurry otherwise, we won't have time to enjoy our champagne before the curtain goes up."

"I'll be selling flowers in the spring, so I'll be sure to give you the best ones if you buy from me again," Penny called after them.

"Don't bother, love. She probably wouldn't even recognise you this time tomorrow." Bernard Ward polished the last few apples on his handcart next to her and chuckled. "Folks like them don't really see us, you know. We probably all look the same to them. You certainly know how to charm the toffs, though; I'll give you that. Must be something to do with your mysterious past." He tapped the side of his nose and gave her a wink.

Penny shook her head. "It's nothing like that.

Maude told me to be polite, that's all." She watched as the wealthy couple greeted some friends who were just dismounting from a gleaming carriage outside the front of the theatre.

"What do you think it would be like to be as wealthy as the toffs, Bernard? Imagine drinking champagne before watching the show. And then dining in one of the fine restaurants afterwards, without even having to think about how much it costs." Her voice sounded wistful as another icy blast of wind whipped through the square, making her teeth chatter.

"You're asking the wrong person," Bernard said, chuckling again. "I've been a lowly costermonger for nigh on fifty years, making just enough to keep the roof over our heads and feed the nine children before they all grew up."

"Don't you like to daydream about having something more?" Penny gave him a curious look.

Maude had arranged for her to stand next to her old friend Bernard on the market square when she first started selling mistletoe two Christmases ago, so he could keep an eye on her. There were plenty of unscrupulous pick-pockets to guard against, and Penny was grateful for his fatherly protection, but she still didn't know much about him.

"Well…there's daydreaming…and then there's hankering after something you can never have," Bernard said thoughtfully. He selected a small apple which had seen better days out of his cart and buffed it on his sleeve before handing it to Penny, who happily nibbled around the bruised part. "The way I see it, if you can find a way to be content with your lot in life, it saves a lot of heartache."

"That's like what Ma says. Having money isn't always the way to be happy. Good friends are what matters more." Penny parroted the words Louisa often murmured but still felt a tug of longing towards the comfort and ease her elegant customers must enjoy. From where she was standing, she could see the woman's jewelled hair combs glinting in the lamplight and hear the well-educated tones of the men as they talked before going up the steps into the cosy interior of the theatre foyer. It was like being given a tiny glimpse into another world. One which Penny could never be part of.

"I don't know about you, but I reckon it's time to pack up and go home, Penny. Have you made enough for the day?" Bernard rubbed his hands together, trying to ease the twinge of arthritis in his gnarly joints. "See you in the morning?"

"I hope so." A shadow crossed Penny's face. "It was true what I said about Ma not being well. That terrible pea-souper fog last week got onto her chest when she was delivering clothes back to the dressmaker. She was coughing something terrible last night even though Maude gave her a spoonful of aniseed balsam."

Bernard gave her a sympathetic smile. Maude had often told him it was a wonder Louisa had recovered on that Christmas eve when Penny had been born.

"The doctor reckoned she wouldn't last until the morning," Maude had confided to him one grey January day when Penny was still a tiny baby. "How she hung on, I'll never know. I think it was only Penny's cries that stopped her from slipping away to the next life. But she'll never regain her full health, Bernard. We just have to hope she can have a few precious years with her baby girl, the poor little mite."

. . .

As Penny hurried home, her thoughts turned towards Bernard's comments about her mysterious past. As far as she knew, it was perfectly straightforward. No secret had been made of the fact that her ma had bumped her head and lost her memory on the night she was born. And they had lived with Maude Bevan and her family ever since. There was certainly no mystery about Penny's life. But she couldn't help but wonder about her ma. Louisa insisted that she still had no recollection of where she had lived before coming to Willow Cottage on Sketty Lane, and sometimes Penny liked to entertain the idea that they came from a wealthy family.

"If you think really hard, Ma, maybe something will come into your mind," Penny had whispered a few nights ago as they were falling asleep. They shared the tiny bedroom under the eaves at the top of Willow Cottage, and even though Louisa discouraged it, Penny loved to suggest different scenarios that might somehow bring the memories flooding back. "What about music? Can you remember dancing in a ball gown? Or horses? Perhaps you had your own horse and used to ride across the land your family owned?"

Louisa had sighed wheezily. "You know that

when Maude found me in the alleyway, my dress was ragged, and my hands were rough. It's a pleasant daydream, Penny, but we have a happy life here. Sometimes it's best to leave the past where it belongs."

"But what if your family are well-to-do, and they've been looking for you all these years?" Penny shivered and pulled the old quilt higher under her chin, trying to imagine a soft feather bed and having enough coal to keep the fire going all night long. "Maude says that you don't sound like someone who came from a poor background."

"We don't want for anything, and Maude has welcomed us into her home. She's all the family we need, even if we're not related by blood. Now, let's go to sleep otherwise, I'll be too tired to get all the mending done for Mrs Washbrook, and you'll be dead on your feet at the market tomorrow."

A GUST of wind snapped Penny back to the present, and she patted her pocket to make sure her earnings were safely hidden away as she rounded the corner into Sketty Lane. She had managed to sell the last few bunches of holly and ivy, although the miserly clerks who'd bought them had beaten down the price. She hoped Maude wouldn't be too disappointed with her takings.

"You're home late tonight." The young barmaid from The Saddlers Arms at the end of the street gave her a cheerful wave. "Keep yer wits around you. The constable has been after a new gang of pickpockets working in this area, apparently."

"Don't worry, Sal, nobody's going to get the better of me." Penny gave the buxom woman a wave as she continued past, glad that they lived on a street where people looked out for each other. Maude liked the occasional bottle of porter, claiming that it helped her rheumatism, and Sal always gave Penny some pickled whelks if there were any going spare when she went to buy the beer.

Haggling with the clerks over her last few bunches of mistletoe had delayed Penny, and she realised that Sal was right. The church clock was already striking six o'clock, and darkness had fallen long ago.

"Just a few more minutes, and I'll be home," Penny muttered to herself. Usually, she didn't mind walking back from the market, but the mention of pickpockets had set her on edge, so she quickened her pace. Suddenly, as if conjured by Sal's comments, a pair of boys appeared out of the shadowy alleyway and blocked her path. They looked to be a couple of years older than Penny and gave her insolent smiles.

"Hand over yer money." The taller of the boys held his hand out, expecting her to comply.

Penny stepped backwards, but as quick as a flash, the other boy darted to her side and grabbed her arm. He grinned again, but this time it had an air of menage. "No need to make this harder than it has to be," he said. "All we want is yer takings, and then we'll be on our way. It's a simple enough request."

The taller boy gazed nonchalantly up and down the street. "Ain't nobody around, so there's no point shouting for help." His shirt hung loosely on his scrawny frame, and there were holes in his shoes.

"Are you the pickpockets the constable is looking for?" Penny retorted, finding her voice. "Sal warned me about you. The constable is probably watching right now, waiting to catch you in the act."

"Oh deary me, we've only gone and chosen someone who thinks they know better than us,

Alf." The boy next to Penny looked down at her with an amused expression.

"So you're called Alf, are you?" Penny said quickly, glaring at the tall boy.

"What did you do that for, Neville?" he shot back, looking annoyed.

"Alf and Neville." Penny shook her head. "You boys aren't very good at this, are you? Now I know both of your names."

"You might think you're smart, but you'll be laughing on the other side of your face if you don't do as we say. Give us yer money, otherwise, you'll regret it."

Penny yelped with pain as the boy called Neville tightened his grip on her arm. He was right, the only light she could see was from the stables in the news, but other than that, the streets seemed deserted. She considered handing the money over but then a surge of anger at the injustice of it all came over her. "Why don't you work for a wage instead of taking it off people like me," she cried. "My ma is ill, and I need every shilling. It's taken me all day to earn a pittance, so why should I give it to you."

"We're not interested in your sob stories," Alf growled. "Besides, selling flowers, or whatever it is you do, is a fool's errand. You should be like us and just take what you want." He snatched her basket and threw it onto the ground before stamping hard on it with his heavy hobnailed boots, not caring about Penny's shocked expression.

"Now do you see that we mean business?" Neville sniggered in her ear.

Penny knew she had no choice. "Let me go, and I'll give you what I have." She glared at Alf again. "I'm not happy about it, though. You should be ashamed of yourselves."

Neville released her, giving her a push that sent her sprawling backwards in the snow. He stood over her and sniggered again, enjoying seeing her fear. "That'll teach you to fight back." He grinned at his accomplice and stuck his thumbs in his ragged waistcoat, looking pleased with himself. "This is a good neighbourhood. Easy pickings. I reckon we'll be seeing more of the people around here, don't you?"

Penny sat up hastily as the cold, wet snow seeped through her dress. Even though she was trying to put on a brave front, her heart was hammering under her ribs, and she just wished they would leave her alone. With trembling fingers, she pulled a couple of coins from the pocket under her apron and held them out. "There you are," she muttered.

"Two coins?" The boys laughed, but there was a cruel edge to it. "Do you take us for fools? You've got more money than that. Now give us all of it, or we'll rip your dress to shreds for every last farthing."

"You'll do no such thing!" A voice rang out in the darkness making the boys spin around.

Penny gasped as she saw a shadow streak across the road from the direction of the stables, followed by the sound of snapping and snarling.

"See 'em off, Turk," the voice commanded. It was swiftly followed by a blood-curdling growl which made the hairs on Penny's arms stand up.

"Get off…let me go," Neville squawked.

"Run, before it bites us." There was genuine fear in Alf's voice as more scuffling ensued.

Penny scrambled to her feet just in time to see her two assailants scurry away back into the alley-way, shrieking with fear, and she looked around anxiously, wondering what beast had sprung from the shadows to save her.

"Are you alright?"

A shaft of moonlight beamed out from the scudding clouds, and Penny found herself face-to-face with another boy. But this time, his freckled face and wide smile reassured her.

"I'm George, and this is Turk, my dog. I don't think those two scoundrels will be bothering you again."

"I…I don't know what to say. Usually, it's quite safe walking home, but this time…" Penny's words petered out as shock took over.

"Have you got much further to go? Turk and I could walk you home if you like. I've just finished feeding the horses. I can do the rest of my jobs a bit later, I expect."

"I only live at Willow Cottage, just a bit further along the lane." Penny glanced nervously up the alley, wanting to say yes, but she didn't want to take up any more of his time. "Won't you be missed?"

George scratched his tousled thatch of brown hair and grinned again. "Well, it's my first day working for the posh family, so I can't rightly say." He gently took hold of Penny's hand and tucked it into the crook of his arm. "But I know Willow Cottage, so I'll have you home in two ticks. What's your name, by the way?" he asked as they set off.

"Penny Frost. It's nice to meet you." She gave him a shy smile as they strolled along the street. He was a couple of inches taller than her, and his warm brown eyes made her feel straight away that she could trust him.

"And you too, Penny." George noticed her looking nervously at the dog. "Turk is a Staffordshire Terrier, if you're wondering. You'll never get a more loyal dog. He's been my best friend since my ma and pa died." The dog gazed up at Penny and wagged his tail. "See, he likes you already. If Turk likes someone, then I do too."

A moment later, they turned into the cobbled courtyard. "This is where I live," Penny said. She wondered whether her new friend would like to come in for a cup of tea.

Just as they reached the cottage, the front door flew open, and Maude appeared, her face wreathed in smiles. "George? You're early. I thought you weren't coming until next week."

Penny looked between the two of them in confusion, wondering how Maude knew the boy.

"This is my nephew," Maude explained. "I meant to tell you that I asked the coachman for the big house if he could have a job, and it clean slipped my mind. How do you know Penny, George?" Her face creased into a frown. "There wasn't any trouble when you were walking home, was there? I heard rumours of a new gang working in this area of town."

George and Penny exchanged a smile. "Nothing that Turk wasn't able to sort out, Aunt Maude."

"Now, you must come in for a cup of tea and tell us all about your new job, George. I know it must have been a wrench when your ma's sister remarried and left to go abroad with her new husband, but I'm sure you'll soon settle in here."

"Maude is my pa's sister," George explained to Penny. When my parents died, I was only three, and my aunt on my mother's side of the family took me in. But she married a tea merchant, and they're going to live in India. They decided it was best for me to stay behind."

"It's their loss," Maude said briskly, sliding the kettle onto the range to boil. She gave him a fond look. "You're the spitting image of my brother, and I can see you're turning into a strapping young lad, even though you're still only eleven. If you work hard for the toffs, who knows where it could lead."

"Where are the twins? And Tom?" George looked around for his cousins. If he wondered why Penny lived there, too, he was too polite to ask.

"They're minding the kilns tonight at the brick-yard. They have to keep the fires stoked, so they don't ever go out, otherwise, Mr Culpepper will be in a high old temper."

Penny hung her shawl behind the door and handed her earnings to Maude. "It was a quiet end to the day, I'm afraid, but I'll try harder tomorrow."

Maude shrugged and took the money gratefully. "Everyone's feeling the pinch, dear. You're doing your best. Why don't you take a cup of tea upstairs for your ma? I sent her to bed early. That cough of hers is getting worse." A shadow of worry clouded her eyes as she watched Penny leave. She had grown as fond of Louisa and her daughter as if they were her own family over the years, but she had a terrible feeling that Louisa might not be much longer for this world.

CHAPTER 4

Penny picked up a handful of soil from the mound left by the gravediggers and leaned forward to drop it onto the cheap wooden coffin that was her ma's last resting place. She had tried hard not to cry, but there was something so final about Louisa's burial that she couldn't hold her emotions back any longer, and hot tears rolled down her cheeks.

"There, there, dear." Maude rested a workworn hand on Penny's shoulder and gave her a sympathetic smile. "I know how difficult this is. Let's go home and get back in the warm again." She had lost half a day's pay for taking time off work to accompany Penny, and Mr Culpepper had been reluctant to agree that everyone deserved a dignified end with a few hours for their loved ones to pay their respects. Maude felt it was a small price to pay to give the girl some support.

Penny gulped and blew her nose, averting her gaze as the gravediggers got to work filling in the grave again. There was no time for lingering farewells in their line of work, especially when the ground was so hard from winter's icy grip that it took twice as long to dig.

Maude steered them back through the graves, pausing only to stand and murmur a few words at the spot where Fred was buried, which was marked with a simple wooden cross. She saw Penny brighten slightly at the thought that her ma was not alone in the church's grounds. "Fred would have liked your ma," she said. "It's a shame they never met but 'tis the way of things. Birth... and then death...we never know how much time the Lord will give us or what the future holds."

"I shall miss her, but I'm glad she's not suffering anymore," Penny said quietly.

In the end, Louisa's demise had been quicker than anyone expected. The cough had rattled ever-louder in her chest, and her skin had taken on a grey pallor that didn't bode well. In spite of the various tonics and compresses that Maude had administered, in the end, there was nothing more to be done.

Penny, my darling...everyone thought I wouldn't even live to see your first birthday. But we've had all these precious years together. Be a good girl...I pray that you will have a happy life and the love of a kindhearted man one day...think of me with fondness...

Louisa's final words to her daughter had been barely above a whisper, but her soft smile had given Penny comfort, and even now, she could hear them in her mind.

"It's a coincidence that your ma and my Fred died at the same time of year as each other," Maude commented as they tramped home through the snow.

"Does it spoil Christmas for you?" Penny asked.

Maude shook her head. "Fred loved all the festivities of Christmas. When he knew he didn't have much longer on this earth, he made me promise not to be gloomy about his passing. 'Light a candle for me, Maudie,' he said, 'and remember me with good cheer for all the happy times we had together,' so that's what I always do."

Penny blew onto her hands and rubbed them together as she thought about what Maude had just said. "Maybe Ma would want me to do the same, do you think? She always said this time of year was extra special because I was born on Christmas eve."

"There you are then. We shall do our best to enjoy ourselves because that's what they would have wanted," Maude replied. "Even better, we'll have George with us this year as well, as long as his master give him the day off."

"He told me that once the horses are taken care of after the family get back from church, he's allowed the rest of the day off." Penny smiled at the thought of having George's company. As much as she loved Tom, Nell, and Jacob, who treated her like a younger sister, she couldn't help but feel that they were closer to one another because of being true siblings. George was slightly more of an outsider within the Bevan family, like her, and even though she had only known him a short time, his irrepressible chatter always lifted her spirits.

A WEEK LATER, Penny ran lightly downstairs and opened the curtains in the small cottage. It was Christmas day, and she was the first person to wake up. The snow was deeper than ever in the cobbled yard outside, lying in soft mounds that were unspoilt from footprints yet. She knelt down in front of the hearth and busied herself with sweeping out the ash so she could rebuild the fire in the grate. Twists of old newspaper, followed by kindling, and then a few lumps of coal. The mindless routine of her morning chores allowed her thoughts to wander, and she realised with relief that it was the first day she hadn't needed to wipe away any tears.

The first few nights after her ma died had felt strange. The bed was too big without Louisa's comforting presence next to her, even though, in reality, it was still the same narrow bedstead and lumpy straw mattress they had always shared.

I'm an orphan now. The thought had consumed her the day after going to the graveyard, but now she had accepted her fate.

Her initial sharp grief had softened into something more manageable, and the comings and goings of the Bevan family helped keep her mood from turning maudlin. The truth was, even at eight years old, Penny knew she was luckier than most other orphans. Many times on her way home from the market, she had picked her way past families cowering in doorways, the children's legs spindly and blue from the cold, clad only in rags. Mothers nursed wailing babies and squabbled over gin and stale crusts, desperate to avoid the dreaded workhouse, while unkempt men who looked more like ghosts than people huddled around meagre fires under the railway arches, eying passers-by with weary resignation.

Yesterday the Bevans had all sung happy birthday to Penny after their evening bowl of stew, and Maude had even produced a lardy cake from her basket with a flourish and told her she didn't have to share it. Except Penny had, of course. Twelve-year-old Jacob seemed to be permanently hungry, and it wouldn't be fair to give him some and ignore Nell.

"Cutting that cake into six won't give you more than a mouthful, Penny. This was meant to be your birthday treat," Maude joked.

Penny had just shrugged as she shared the rare sweet treat around. "I wouldn't enjoy eating it, knowing that I was the only one. At least this way, the day feels a bit special for all of us."

Maude had smacked Tom's hand away as it hovered over the final piece. "That's for George, you greedy thing. The sooner you set off to sea, the better." Her eyes had misted over even as she said it. Tom had been accepted to work on one of the many clippers that sailed from Cardiff docks to the Spice Islands after pleading with Maude to let him follow his dream of being a sailor. The last few days had seen a flurry of preparation as he assembled his belongings to take to sea with him, whistling loudly and filling the cottage with jaunty renditions of sea shanties as his excitement grew. Ever since the captain had sent a message to say they would raise anchor on the first calm day with a suitable tide, Maude alternated between stifled sobs about how much she would miss her eldest son and worried frowns about how they would manage without his wage coming in any longer from working at the brickyards.

Penny glanced at the clock on the mantel shelf. It was still early, so she had plenty of time to dust and polish. After eating his portion of the lardy cake the night before, Tom had gently broken the news that he would be leaving in a couple of days' time, which made it all the more important for them to enjoy this day, and she wanted to make it nice for Maude.

. . .

"MERRY CHRISTMAS, EVERYONE!" George's jovial shout came late in the morning, and Penny hurried to the door to let him in. "Look what the master gave me." He held up a brace of rabbits as he came in, stamping the snow off his feet.

"That's very generous of him," Maude said, happily taking them off him.

"Well, they were really meant to be for Mr Webster, the head coachman, but his wife said that eating rabbits is common, and since he got promoted from being a lowly groom, they should be dining on beef."

"All the better for us," Nell said, pulling a face. "Common? Whoever heard of such a thing? Those rabbits will last us in a stew for the best part of a week if Penny gets plenty of vegetables from Bernard to add to the pot."

"Mrs Webster is full of airs and graces," George commented. He gave Penny an extravagant bow as he unwound his scarf, making her giggle. "'Don't bring mud into the house, Percival'," he mimicked in a fluting voice. "'Make sure that the new boy washes his hands'." He stuck his nose up into the air and flounced past as though he was wearing a gown, making Penny laugh even harder.

"Abigail always did have delusions of

grandeur," Maude said. Her plump shoulders shook with amusement at George's impersonations. "She's born and bred in the poor end of Brynwell, just like the rest of us, but when Percy got a job for the toffs, you'd have thought it was like working for Queen Victoria herself, the way she suddenly started thinking herself better than everyone else."

"I don't mind," George said goodnaturedly. "She's too busy decorating their new house at the end of the mews to bother us stable lads, and if Mr Webster hadn't been promoted, I might never have got the job and been able to come and live so close to you all…or met Penny."

Penny felt a warm glow on her cheeks as he winked at her.

After a final rush of activity in the kitchen, they all sat at the scrubbed wooden table, which was adorned with the last few sprigs of holly and ivy that had been too blemished to sell, despite Penny's best efforts. She was glad there were a few left over because, with the flickering candles, the table looked more festive than she'd ever seen it before.

"Roast beef…I'm so hungry I've been dreaming about this for days," Jacob sighed, gazing longingly at the joint of meat that Maude carefully placed at the head of the table.

"And carrots, cabbage, roast potatoes and gravy." Penny and Nell carried the vegetables to the table, their mouths watering already.

Maude sharpened the knife on a steel and carved thin slices of the succulent meat before everyone helped themselves to the accompaniments. She had been squirrelling away a few coins every week for the last few months so they could enjoy Christmas, and although she knew they would have to be more frugal in the new year, it was worth it to see the pleasure on everyone's faces.

"To absent friends," Tom said after they had eaten their fill and Maude had allowed them all a small glass of wine.

Penny felt a pang of sadness as she thought about her ma, but a moment later, George reached under the table and squeezed her hand, giving her a warm smile. She blinked back the tears which pricked the back of her eyes. "Ma would have enjoyed this very much. Thank you for such a wonderful day, Maude."

"Time for plum pudding and then carols," Nell said, jumping up.

"I think this is the best Christmas I've ever had," George said, giving Penny's hand another squeeze.

"We do, too," everyone chorused.

"And don't forget the presents." As soon as they had finished eating and were feeling sleepily full, Tom handed out the parcels which had been nestling under the boughs of evergreen foliage Maude had artfully arranged on the sideboard in place of a Christmas tree, which they couldn't afford.

They each carefully removed the brown paper that was wrapped around their gifts. A new handkerchief for the girls, embroidered with their initials, and knitted socks for the boys.

The rest of the afternoon passed all too quickly as they gathered in front of the crackling fire to sing carols and read aloud from the small selection of books that took pride of place next to the chair where Fred always used to sit. As darkness fell early outside and the snow settled deeper on the ground, Penny sighed happily. She had been dreading her first Christmas without her dear ma, but the cosiness of Willow Cottage and the company of her adopted family had made the day more wonderful than she could have imagined.

"Did you enjoy yourself?" Maude asked as she

tucked Penny up under her old patchwork quilt later that night.

Penny's eyelids were already growing heavy with sleep. "I think it was wonderful. I wish everything would always stay just like this."

Maude brushed a kiss on Penny's forehead and pulled something from her dress pocket. "I have something I need to show you, dear. Your ma asked me to tell you about this and then give it to you when you're older."

Penny sat up, wide awake again. "What is it?"

"You know she had nothing to her name when she arrived other than one penny, which was why you have the name you do. And we never knew Louisa's surname, so Tom suggested Frost because it was such a bitterly cold night, and the idea stuck."

Penny nodded. Louisa had often told her that story, and she smiled at hearing it again.

"What we never told you is that she did have something else. She was wearing this brooch on the collar of her dress when I found her in the snow the night that you were born." Maude passed it to Penny.

"It's beautiful," Penny whispered. She held it up to the light of her night candle to see it more clearly. It was a delicate oval shape, fashioned out of silver with a mother-of-pearl dove inlaid at the centre that shimmered slightly as it caught the light. "And you say Ma was wearing it?"

"Yes, dear." Maude's expression softened. "I think it may hold some sort of link to your ma's past, but she never said what it might be. Whether it was because she couldn't remember or she didn't want to think about it, I never could tell. But when she got sick a few weeks ago, she said that I was to show it to you and then look after it for safe-keeping until you turn eighteen."

Penny folded the brooch into her hands and pressed it to her chest as tears pooled in her eyes. "Now I'll always have something to remember Ma by."

"Why don't you sleep with it under your pillow tonight, and then we'll put it somewhere safe tomorrow morning?" Maude pulled the quilt under Penny's chin as the silvery moon rose in the sky, casting a soft glow on her brown curls that were fanned across the pillow.

"Do you really think this holds the secret to my past?" Penny murmured. She felt a shiver of something she couldn't quite name at her tender age. Was it excitement at the idea of a mysterious past that she might one day discover? Or trepidation that it might take her away from the only people she knew as family, even though they weren't related?

"Whatever happens in the future, I want you to know that you'll always have a home with us, Penny. It might not be grand, but we think of you as part of our family and always will."

Maude sighed as the watched the conflicting thoughts flit across Penny's brown eyes just before they closed. She wanted the best for the girl, but she was worried that the brooch might lead to something that could bring no good.

CHAPTER 5

"Can't you work any faster? I'm not paying you to stand around warming your hands." Ernest Culpepper gave Penny a steely look. There was a glint of satisfaction in his eyes as he saw her jump at the sound of his voice.

"I'm sorry, Mr Culpepper. It's just that my hands are so cold that it's hard to pick the wet bricks up properly."

"Excuses, excuses." Culpepper folded his arms across his chest and walked around Penny shaking his head slightly. "If you're cold, you should work harder. That'll soon make you feel warmer." His own gaunt cheeks were tinged with purple, and his eyes were bloodshot. Penny could only assume that the regular nips of rum he took from his hip flask when he thought nobody was looking made him impervious to the weather as he looked the same no matter what time of year it was.

A biting wind whistled through the yard of the brickworks, blowing straight off the sea, carrying with it tiny crystals of ice. Somewhere between hailstones and snowflakes, as though the dank harbour fog had frozen, it felt like being stung by pinpricks every time Penny walked from the cavernous shed where the master brickmakers shaped the bricks to the collecting area where they were stacked to await the drying process.

Back and forth, dozens of times a day, from dawn until dusk, Penny and the other workers trudged, lugging their hack barrows, loaded up with newly moulded bricks that were still in the form of wet clay. She had started working at Culpepper's brickyard just after Tom had left to go to sea, and it was hard to believe she had been there almost six years. At the end of each day, her muscles burned with weariness, and her hands were rough from the hard labour.

"Remind me how old you are, child?" Mr Culpepper looked her up and down, taking in the new womanly curves under her shapeless brown woollen dress.

Penny tightened her shawl, not liking the way he was eying her up like a beast at market. "I'll be fourteen years old in a few weeks. Why do you ask?"

He looked irritated that she was questioning him back. "You should be capable of carrying more bricks if that's your age. I rue the day Maude let that son of hers leave to work on the ships. A fine, strapping lad, Tom was. And to think, she persuaded me that you would make up for it."

"Is there a problem, Mr Culpepper?" Maude bustled over with a worried frown on her face.

"Just the usual, Mrs Bevan," he snapped. "Penny here seems to think that it's perfectly acceptable to warm her hands by the kiln as if we had all the time in the world to complete today's order of bricks for Sir Calder."

"I'm sure it was just for a second," Maude said hastily. "Penny works every bit as hard as Jacob and Nell."

"That's debatable. Your own children are made of sturdier stuff, Mrs Bevan, whereas Penny often seems to be daydreaming whenever I see her."

"I've fulfilled my numbers every day for the last month, Mr Culpepper. What you're saying isn't true." Penny knew she should meekly accept his comments, but she couldn't help but defend herself. Ever since she had started working here, he had taken a dislike to her. His favourite way of showing it was to point out her shortcomings compared to the rest of the Bevan family. Like most brickyards, working here was a closed shop, with jobs usually only offered to other family members. It was only because Tom had left to become a sailor that Penny had been allowed to take his place. A fact that Culpepper liked to remind her of regularly.

Mr Culpepper gave her a triumphant smile. "Thank you for reminding me, Penny. In that case, what with you turning fourteen soon, I shall increase your quota in the new year."

"But you already increased it in the summer—"

Culpepper held up a bony hand to stop Penny from saying anything else. "Sir Henry Calder is working with one of London's finest architects to build a new orangery at Talbot Manor. It will be the envy of the nation, and people will travel all the way from the city to come and admire it, I don't doubt. Would you like me to tell him that the building works might fall behind schedule because my workers are idly warming themselves by the kiln? Or that they refuse to take on extra work?"

"I'm sure Penny meant to say that we'll be only too happy to do more, Mr Culpepper." Two bright spots of colour had appeared on Maude's cheeks as she gave him an ingratiating smile.

"It has also been most inconvenient having to take on a new clerk since Mr Bevan died," he continued. His thin lips were pinched with irritation. "It was only out of a sense of charity that I allowed your family to remain in your cottage on Sketty Lane."

"I know," Maude said hastily. "And we're truly grateful, sir."

Penny felt a stab of guilt at the way Maude had to grovel to keep Mr Culpepper happy. It wasn't right, but they had no choice. "I'm sorry. I'll be only too happy to meet the increased amount after my birthday," she said, giving their employer the pretty smile she had used all the time when selling flowers at the market. It seemed to do the trick.

"Very well. I'm glad you remembered your place, Miss Frost. There are plenty of other families who would be delighted to live in your cottage, but Sir Henry does have the quaint notion of not making his workers homeless...even when they're insubordinate."

Maude practically curtsied with relief. "We

never take your generosity for granted, Mr Culpepper. That's why my Fred worked all the hours he could when he was your clerk, right up until he couldn't get out of bed with his pneumonia."

Culpepper sniffed and gave her a curt nod. "As it should be, Mrs Bevan. As it should be. Fred understood the meaning of hard work to further the success of our little brickworks…something you'd be wise to instil in the rest of your family and Miss Frost. If everything goes to plan with the orangery, Sir Henry hopes to be able to expand the brickworks so we can supply even more bricks to other customers."

Penny tried not to let her resentment show as she hurried away to fetch her next load of bricks. Culpepper thought nothing of making them continue working long after they were supposed to go home. And he even got around the new employment laws that banned children from working there by claiming that the parents brought their children to the yards so they wouldn't be left alone at home.

"It's out of my hands," she overheard him saying to the inspectors. "They bring their children, bless them, and who am I to say they should shiver in the cold rather than keep warm by helping carry the occasional brick? It would be very unchristian of me to turn the little ones away."

As soon as the inspectors had left, he had chivied all the children back to their usual tasks, fetching and carrying the wet bricks without a care for the dark circles of exhaustion under their eyes or the risk that their young limbs might become deformed from the heavy loads they grappled with every day.

"Not long until hometime," she murmured, smiling to encourage two six-year-old children as they staggered past, pushing a barrow load of wet clay to keep the master brickmakers supplied with their raw materials.

If I was in charge, I'd make sure the children were at school, and the workers had proper breaks. The familiar thought filled her mind again and Penny gave Maude a rueful smile as she caught her eye. Maude knew Penny's views and often had to remind her that families like the Bevans had to accept things as they were.

Her muscles twinged as she loaded up a new barrow with bricks, working fast to keep up with the men who had perfected their craft over many years.

"I 'ope they let us visit this 'ere orangery when it's made," one of the men muttered as he deftly slapped the wet clay into its wooden mould before scraping the excess off in one smooth sweep with his striker.

Penny could only nod in agreement. As she trotted back and forth between the sheds for the rest of the day, she allowed her mind to wander and daydream, which was one of her favourite pastimes. She imagined herself in the back of a gleaming carriage, dressed in a sprigged muslin gown, drawing up outside the ornate front of Talbot Manor. With each new load of bricks, her daydream grew more fanciful...tea on the lawn with peacocks in the background...gardeners bringing her fragrant blooms to arrange in a cut glass vase...a handsome gentleman in a top hat bowing low to kiss the back of her hand. It helped her while away the dreary hours until darkness fell, and they could walk back through the snowy streets to their home for a warming cup of tea.

"I HAVE A SURPRISE FOR YOUR BIRTHDAY." George produced a parcel wrapped in brown paper from under his coat and handed it to Penny as Maude smiled from where she was standing next to the range stirring a bubbling pan of stew.

"Did you know he was going to do this?" Penny asked, turning pink. "I thought we agreed not to bother with presents this year, what with money being so tight."

George shrugged with a twinkle in his eye. "I don't remember anyone saying that."

"Oh, it's beautiful, George, thank you." Penny peeled back the paper and then hugged the soft, woollen scarf against her cheek before wrapping it around her neck. The deep, ruby colour of the wool set off her brown hair to perfection, and she knew she would treasure it forever, not least because it was from her favourite person.

"George saved up to buy the wool, and I knitted it for him." Maude swept Penny into an embrace and then presented her with a matching pair of mittens. "I'm afraid it's your Christmas present as well, so I hope you don't mind?"

"Of course not," Penny said, hugging Maude back. "It's far more than I dreamt of having."

"You'll need to wrap up warmly because that's

not all. I'm taking you out for the afternoon," George added.

Penny's eyes widened with curiosity as she saw Maude and George exchanging a glance. "This is very mysterious. Are you going to tell me where we're going?"

"All will be revealed soon enough," George chuckled, tapping the side of his nose. "Just make sure you have your cloak on, as it's perishing cold out there today. We'll leave after we've had a cup of tea."

"There's one more thing." Maude pulled her carved wooden sewing box down from the small nook next to the chimney where it lived and opened one of the compartments inside. "As it's your birthday, why don't you wear your ma's brooch for a treat? I think she would have liked that."

A mixture of emotions welled up inside Penny as Maude carefully pinned the silver brooch to the collar of her dress. "Are you sure it's alright? Didn't Ma want me to wait until I'm eighteen?"

"You've worked hard these last few months in spite of what that old miser Mr Culpepper said the other day. I don't see why you shouldn't wear it for best now and again."

"It's lovely, Penny. Look in the mirror." Nell jumped up from the chair by the fire where she had been mending an apron and propelled Penny to stand in front of the fly-speckled mirror that hung by the door. "The mother of pearl is so delicate. Do you think the dove signifies something to do with love? Maybe it was from your papa…her sweetheart?" she asked breathlessly.

"I'll never know. Ma didn't ever reveal who my father was." Penny felt a pang of regret, but then Nell adjusted a hair comb that held her curls in place, and the moment passed. Nell had just started walking out with the baker's son, and Penny smiled at the way her head was full of nothing but romance. "I'm just grateful to have something that belonged to her," she added stoutly. "It doesn't matter what it signified, just that I have it."

"Shall we be on our way then?" George gulped his cup of tea down and then held Penny's cloak out gallantly for her. "We'll be home before dark, Aunt Maude, and don't worry, I'll take good care of her." His tone was mischievous because Maude always wanted to make sure her brood was safe when they went out.

Maude swished him with her tea towel. "Less of

your cheek, George. Penny's turning into a beautiful young lady, and I don't want her attracting the wrong sort of attention."

"I don't think George would let any other young men have a look in, Ma," Jacob piped up as he appeared in the doorway wrestling an armful of pine tree foliage. He winked as Penny blushed, and Maude rolled her eyes in mock horror. "What?" he added, with a chuckle. "I know Penny's only fourteen, but one day in the future, they'll make the perfect couple."

This time it was George's turn to blush as they hurried past Jacob. "What a lot of nonsense my cousin speaks," he muttered. "Now, shall we get started on your birthday surprise?"

"Come on, Turk." Penny stroked the dog's broad head, and his tail wagged faster, thumping against her leg. Second only to George, Turk was devoted to Penny, and she couldn't believe that she had once thought him frightening.

The low winter sun glinted off the icicles which hung from the eaves of the cottages as they set out, and Penny was grateful for her new scarf and mittens. As the fresh snow creaked under their boots with each footstep and Turk trotted on ahead of them, her thoughts turned to what Jacob had just said. She had always considered George to be her best friend ever since the day he and Turk had rescued her from being attacked, but lately, her heart fluttered in a different and unexpected way when he called around to the cottage. Now that he was almost seventeen years old, and with the hard work in the stables, his shoulders had broadened, and he had a muscular physique. She noticed that young ladies often turned to stare, then looked away with rosy cheeks. He was not good-looking in the way that some of the well-to-do gentlemen of town were, with their finely cut suits and confident swagger that came from wealth and a sense of entitlement. Instead, his features were rugged but kind, and there was something about George's warm brown eyes that had started to make Penny daydream about the very thing that Jacob had hinted at…a future with him as her husband.

"We're going in here first." George turned into the mews, much to Penny's surprise.

"Do you still have some work to do with the horses? I'd love to see what you do, but I've never dared call by in case Mr Webster told me off."

"No, I've finished my jobs for the day, and you'll be pleased to know that the place is deserted." George grinned. "The Websters are enjoying an afternoon off, as are most of the maids, because the master is busy entertaining his new bride-to-be in London, apparently. Even the butler is away visiting his sister for the day."

Penny felt a sudden thrill of excitement. "You mean I can look around? I've always wondered what Melbury House is really like, but it's impossible to see much from Sketty Lane. I'm not sure I even know much about the Calder family, considering you've worked for them for all this time."

He beckoned her towards the stables, and Penny hurried after him, happy that she would be able to imagine George when he was working. "This is where all the horses are kept, as you can see. I sleep up there in the hayloft with the two other grooms, and that small house at the end of the courtyard is where Mr and Mrs Webster live."

Penny was drawn to the horses as they munched their hay. Each one had its own stall, and even with her inexperienced eye, she could tell that they were well-bred animals, a world apart from the sturdy, rough-coated cobs that clopped through town pulling the wagons for the local draymen and traders.

"Lovely, aren't they?" George murmured. He

reached over the railings and patted the neck of a stunning dappled grey horse. "I still can't believe how lucky I am to have this job. I always wanted to work with horses, and I hope that one day I might even become head coachman when Percy retires."

"You seem so confident around them," Penny commented. She could tell that the horses liked George by the way their ears flicked forward, and they looked at him with their liquid brown gaze as he talked to them in a low voice.

"You know where you are with horses," he chuckled. "If you do something wrong, they'll soon let you know. Shall we go and look at the garden now?"

Penny nodded, although her heart was in her mouth. "What if we get caught?" she whispered.

"You'll be fine; just stick close to me."

A moment later, Penny found herself in a charming walled garden. Even under the snow, she could see that the beds had pleasing symmetry and were well-tended. There were espaliered fruit trees trained against the shelter of the red-brick walls and a rose arbour at the centre, with pathways leading off like the spokes of a cartwheel.

At the far end of the garden was the house itself, and beyond it, she could see a sweeping gravelled driveway for the carriage to collect the family. Even though Melbury House was within Brynwell town, it felt like entering a different world, away from the rumbling wagons on the lanes and the hustle and bustle of people walking to and from their place of work. It was like a quiet, elegant oasis of calmness and understated wealth, and Penny felt a sudden overwhelming wish that she could live there.

"This is the most beautiful place I've ever seen," Penny whispered, her eyes shining as she turned to smile at George. "Imagine if it was ours, George. We would take tea in the garden in summer, and Maude and Nell and Jacob would never have to work at those wretched brickyards for another day."

"It's a lovely dream," George chuckled. "Maybe you could see about working here as a maid? Everyone likes Sir Calder. He seems rather easy-going and lets the housekeeper and butler manage the place, although I'm sure things might change a bit if his new wife comes to live here."

Penny's face fell. "I don't think Mr Culpepper would ever let me go. He's always complaining that we're too short of workers as it is."

"Never mind...we can pretend just for this

afternoon." George bowed over Penny's hand. "Would you allow me to show you the Christmas decorations, Miss Frost? I think you'll find them quite delightful."

They picked their way carefully through the garden, and then George led her to some tall windows that overlooked an ornamental pond. "This is the drawing room," he said in a low voice. "Sir Henry asked us to take the Christmas tree in there the other day. Would you like to see it?"

Penny placed her mittened hands against the glass and peeked into the room. What she saw within made her smile with astonishment. "It's almost as tall as the tree at the centre of the market square," she gasped. The spruce fir tree stood in the corner of an elegant room and was adorned with more glass baubles and ribbons of tinsel than she had ever seen in her life, as well as having a glittering star at the top, and candles on every bough. She imagined a fire crackling in the hearth and each candle twinkling in the soft evening lamplight. But that wasn't all. There were also swags of ivy and evergreen fronds woven between the ornaments on almost every surface of the gleaming mahogany furniture and a mound of gifts on the sideboard, each one exquisitely wrapped in colourful paper and velvet ribbon bows.

"It's quite something to behold, isn't it," George said, raising his eyebrows.

"Does Sir Henry have a large family? There are enough presents there for the whole street."

George shook his head. "No. Quite the opposite. Sir Henry's previous wife passed away a few years ago. Rumour has it that the woman he intends to marry in the new year has children, but none of us has met them yet. She lives in London at the moment."

Penny pressed her nose to the window and looked around the rest of the room, wanting to commit every detail of the luxurious interior to her memory so she could daydream about it later on. There was a large bookcase along one wall, lined with leather-bound books, and a piano with sheet music propped up above the keys as though someone had recently been playing. In front of the cavernous hearth was a brightly coloured Persian rug, and there were exotic hothouse flowers arranged in a vase on top of the escritoire.

"That's the family, there." George pointed towards a painting in an ornate gold frame hanging in the corner of the room, and Penny looked at it intently.

"Sir Henry looks kind, and his wife is beautiful." The painting showed a tall man with a patrician bearing standing next to an armchair in which an elegant, dark-haired woman was sitting. She looked younger than him by a few years, and there was a little girl sitting at the foot of the chair, playing with a small King Charles spaniel.

"The housekeeper told me that Lady Calder was often unwell. She preferred this house, but it's where she became sick, which is why Sir Henry doesn't spend much time here and prefers to be at Talbot Manor which is far grander, by all accounts. It's only because he's making improvements to the manor house for his new wife that he's been staying here recently."

Penny shook her head in wonder that someone should own a place as lovely as Melbury House and not want to be there all the time. "What of the girl in the picture?" she asked, looking at it again. There was something about the way the artist had captured the girl that struck a chord with her, even though the style of her gown showed that it had been painted some years before.

"Their daughter, I believe." George's words

were whispered this time. He glanced over his shoulder. "I was told the day I first started working here that she's never to be mentioned—"

Just as Penny was about to press him for more detail, the sound of squabbling voices erupted across from the servant's entrance.

"Cook's got it in for the scullery maid, which means she'll be in a bad mood," George said, grabbing Penny's hand. "We'd better leave now. Besides, we need plenty of time for the next part of your surprise." They ran through the garden back towards the stable block, and Turk gambolled ahead with an excited bark, glad to be on the move again.

CHAPTER 6

"What do you think? Shall we give it a go?" George gave Penny a hesitant smile, suddenly worried that she might not like his plan as they surveyed the frozen river and swooping figures skating past in front of them.

Penny clapped her hands and beamed with excitement. "Of course! It looks so much fun, although I might not be very good at it. I've never skated before."

They stood for a moment, watching everyone. There were matronly ladies, cautiously stepping onto the ice, only to be transformed into looking like elegant swans gliding gently forward a moment later, and gaggles of children whooping with joy as they weaved in between the other skaters. Couples twirled together, arm in arm, their scarves streaming out behind them, and the air was filled with laughter.

George jingled the coins in his pocket. "We can hire skates from the gentleman over there, and hopefully, we'll have enough left over to buy some gingerbread and a mug of hot chocolate afterwards."

"I think this is the best birthday I've ever had, George, and it's all thanks to you." Penny smiled up at him, noticing the way the winter sun lit up the flecks of hazel in his brown eyes.

The tips of his ears turned pink, and he shrugged her words away. "I know you always miss your ma more at this time of year. It's the least I could do for my best friend." He steered her towards the stall that had skates of all sizes piled up on it. "Two pairs of skates, please, sir."

For the next hour, Penny felt as free as a bird. It was as though all her worries about keeping Mr Culpepper happy and earning enough money to help keep the cottage for Maude were thrown off, and she could just enjoy George's company without a care in the world. Once she had got the hang of balancing on the narrow blades, Penny discovered that the secret to staying upright was to keep moving.

"Follow me," George called, zig-zagging away in front of her. His skates hissed as they carved through the ice, and she tried not to think about the frigid dark water of the river beneath them. It had been such a long spell of cold temperatures that the man hiring out the skates had assured them there was no chance of the ice cracking.

Penny kept her gaze firmly on George so as not to be distracted by the thought of crashing into anyone else, and much to her surprise, she quickly changed from feeling as hesitant and wobbly as a new-born foal to swooping along the ice next to him with exhilarating ease. Their breath plumed above them in the crisp December air, and her cheeks turned rosy pink, making her look so beautiful that it was hard for George to take his eyes off her.

By the time the winter sky started to turn pale pink as the sun dipped below the rooftops, Penny's feet were aching from the tightly laced skate boots, and she knew her toes would be sore the following day. She heard the church bells chime and saw George wave and turn to come towards her. Their hour was up, and it was time for them to return their skates, otherwise, they would have to pay extra.

Before Penny had a chance to get off the ice, she suddenly noticed a portly gentleman with a worried expression attempting to launch himself from the wooden platform at the riverbank.

"Mind out!" he spluttered. "Wretched skates... what a ridiculous pastime." His arms windmilled wildly as he attempted some jerky steps on the ice and slid towards Penny with a look of intense concentration.

"Go faster, dear," his wife called. She glided next to him, and he shot her a look of irritation.

"Alright," he snapped. "If you could just stop fussing, Mildred, this would be much easier." He teetered forward and suddenly seemed to gather momentum. "Out of my way, girl," he shouted, but it was too late.

Penny felt as though all the air had been punched out of her lungs as the man barrelled into her, sending her crashing over onto the hard ice.

"Sorry," he mumbled as he wobbled onwards, quite unable to stop himself to check that she was alright.

She blinked as black spots clouded her vision, rubbing the side of her head.

"Penny! Are you hurt?" George swooped towards her, looking alarmed. "I lost sight of you, and the next thing I saw was that rude man barging into you and knocking you over. Have you hurt yourself? Let me help you up."

Penny felt his strong hands under her arms, and the next thing she knew, he was lifting her upright as though she was as light as a feather. She wobbled again, feeling suddenly overwhelmed by the moment. Whether it was from the shock of such a hard fall, or the sensation of George's muscular arms encircling her, she wasn't sure.

"I…I'm fine now," she stammered. She looked up into George's brown eyes, seeing him as the handsome man he had become, and for one dizzying moment, it felt as though they were the only people on the frozen river.

"I was worried when I couldn't see you," George said softly. He brushed a lock of hair off her forehead and then lowered his head, pressing the lightest of kisses on her cheek. "What would I do without you, Penny?"

She felt her pulse quicken as the first stirrings of love took seed in her heart and smiled up at him again, feeling suddenly shy in a way she never had before. "Thank you for rescuing me again," she said, touching her cheek where his warm lips had been a moment before, wanting to savour the moment.

"I'll never let anyone hurt you, Penny," he said. He took a deep breath, and his hands lingered on her shoulders. "When we're older...do you think..."

Penny's heart skipped a beat as she saw something new in George's gaze that hinted at something more than just the childlike friendship which had bound them since that fateful day when he and Turk had burst into her life. "Do I think what?" she whispered.

"Oy! Are you bringing those skates back or hiring them for another hour?" The strident voice of the man on the bank shattered the moment of intimacy, and Penny slid backwards out of the delightful safety of George's arms, her cheeks suddenly aflame with embarrassment that the man had been watching.

"Let's get off the river and have a hot chocolate, shall we?" George said lightly. "I'm starving hungry, and I reckon you'll need a hot compress on your bruises if you're going to be able to walk tomorrow. I hope Maude doesn't tell me off," he added with a chuckle.

Penny followed George towards the bank, feeling torn between wanting to be back in his arms again and not knowing what to think of these new emotions that she was experiencing as she felt herself hovering on the brink of becoming a young woman with all the confusing hopes and passions that entailed.

ONCE THEY HAD their own boots back on again, George tucked Penny's hand into the crook of his arm, and they strolled companionably around the stalls of the Winter Fayre that were dotted along the lane next to the river. Brightly dressed performers juggled with flaming torches, and vendors called out to try and sell their wares.

The aroma of sweet ginger and cinnamon made Penny's mouth water as George handed over a coin for two slices of the sticky cake, which they ate with relish, washing it down with a steaming mug of hot chocolate.

Penny's cheeks were still flushed from ice skating, and she opened her cloak to cool off as they stood to admire a troupe of acrobats. A crowd had gathered, and there were gasps of admiration as the swarthy men and lithe women from the troupe balanced on each other's shoulders in impossible feats of agility and strength, despite the snow under their feet.

"Good afternoon, George. I didn't realise you were coming here this afternoon."

The voice startled Penny as she had been mesmerised by watching the performance. She turned to see a couple standing behind them. They were smartly dressed, and she wondered who they were.

"Hello, Mr Webster." George lifted his cap. "And good afternoon to you too, Mrs Webster."

"Did you finish feeding all the horses?" Percy Webster asked.

Penny realised it was the head coachman from Melbury House with his wife and hastily patted her hair to try and tame her curls. She wanted to make a good impression on George's boss.

"Yes, and I fetched extra hay, so there will be less to do tomorrow, just as you told me to do."

Mr Webster nodded, seemingly satisfied. "In that case, I suppose it's alright for you to have an hour or two off as long as you don't make a habit of it. I don't want you setting a bad example to the younger boys."

"I made sure that Bobby and Ned mucked out

all the stalls properly. They're good boys, Mr Webster, and you know how grateful they were to be taken on from the orphanage."

Abigail Webster gave Penny a prim look, and she hoped that the woman hadn't witnessed what had just happened on the ice.

"Who is this young lady with you, George?" she asked pointedly

"I'm Miss Frost," Penny said hurriedly. "Penny Frost…a sort of cousin of George's."

"I see. Although I'm not sure how a person can be a sort of cousin," Abigail said, repeating Penny's words without smiling. Unlike Mr Webster, who was plump, she was small and angular, with a thin face and pointed nose. Her eyes darted this way and that as though she was constantly on guard. "I'm not sure I approve of the costumes those performers are wearing," she said, eying the acrobats suspiciously. "The women look terribly vulgar," she added with a disparaging sniff.

Mr Webster nodded in agreement, although secretly Penny thought he seemed rather taken with the ladies in their revealing sequined outfits. She remembered how Maude had mentioned that Abigail Webster considered herself rather superior to the other working-class folk in the neighbourhood, and now that she had met the shrew-like woman for herself, she was inclined to agree.

"You were explaining how you're not quite George's cousin," Abigail continued, turning back to look at Penny with raised eyebrows.

"Oh...was I? What I meant is that George's aunt took me in when I was a baby," Penny murmured.

"I see," Abigail said again. "From the orphanage? Or somewhere else?"

Penny was starting to feel flustered at Mrs Webster's questions. She didn't want to explain how Maude had found her ma in the snow all those years ago, and she felt George step slightly closer as though to protect her from the woman's nosy interest.

"It...it wasn't the orphanage...she just...helped my ma when she was down on her luck," Penny stuttered. Mr and Mrs Webster were far senior to George in the hierarchy of staff at Melbury House, and she didn't want to get him into trouble by not replying. She could feel her cheeks turning red and a headache starting to pound behind her eyes from where she had bumped her head on the ice, and she hastily untied the scarf around her neck to cool herself.

"Very interesting." Mrs Webster's gaze roamed over Penny's dark curls, which framed her oval-shaped face and suddenly came to a stop as she spotted the brooch on her collar. "What a charming trinket," she said, stepping closer.

Penny wished she hadn't loosened her scarf, but it was too late. The woman's hand shot out, and she grasped Penny's collar to get a better look at the brooch.

"It belonged to my ma," Penny said, filled with a surge of pride. They might have come from humble beginnings, but she would never let anyone make her feel as though her ma was worthless. "Maude let me wear it today because it's my birthday. It's a very special brooch."

"I can see why. The mother of pearl dove is very sweet, and as you say, all the more special that it was a gift from your mama." Mrs Webster was suddenly all smiles as she looked around the milling crowds. "Is she here with you? Your mama? It would be nice to meet her. Mr Webster and I always like to take an interest in the families of the boys who work in the stables."

"Penny's mother passed away a few years ago," George said. He put his arm around Penny's shoulder.

"Such a terrible shame, my dear," Mrs Webster said. "And to think, you've been George's sort of cousin all this time, and we never knew either you or your mama. I'm surprised we didn't see her out and about in Brynwell."

"She had to stay inside when her health got worse. The damp weather didn't agree with her, and she preferred to work indoors." Penny wondered whether she had misjudged Abigail as she nodded sympathetically with her head tilted slightly to one side.

"What a lovely gesture for your guardian to let you wear this brooch for your birthday. How old did you say you were today?" Abigail patted Penny on the arm as she looked at the brooch again. Her small dark eyes and the way she tilted her head slightly to one side made Penny think she looked like a small bird.

"I'm fourteen years old. I work at Culpepper's brickworks with Maude and her family, and Maude has always been very kind looking after me."

Abigail exchanged a glance with her husband that was hard to read. "Maude Bevan, you say? She is such a lovely woman with a heart of gold, although I haven't seen her for years. Well, we'll let you get on your way and enjoy the rest of the entertainment. Do you have far to walk home?"

"Only to the cottages along the way from the mews," George said. He tipped his cap again. "We'd better get back before my aunt wonders where we are. She doesn't like Penny to stay out too late with so many pickpockets and ne'er-do-wells on the streets after dark."

"Very wise of her," Mrs Webster said. "You never know what sort of harm a young lady might come to."

In the time they had been speaking, the sun had set, and darkness had fallen over Brynwell. The last few ice skaters were returning their skates, and the lamplighter was out, whistling loudly as he ran up and down his ladder to light the gaslamps along the street.

"Did you enjoy the afternoon?" George said. "I'm sorry if Mrs Webster seemed overbearing with her questions. She's terribly nosy, which is why I try not to have much to do with her, but I have to keep on her good side."

"I expect she was just being friendly," Penny said, already putting the encounter from her mind. "It was a perfectly wonderful day, and better still, we still have Christmas day to look forward to tomorrow."

"You always think the best of people, Penny Frost. Did you know that's one of the many things I like about you?"

She smiled up at George, feeling a renewed flutter of emotion in her chest at his kind words. They had been friends for as long as she could remember, but now she felt something more... perhaps Jacob and Nell were right in the way they already thought she and George would make the ideal couple one day.

Glancing over her shoulder, she saw Mr and Mrs Webster watching them with thoughtful expressions. She lifted her hand a waved goodbye.

"Maybe Mrs Webster would put in a good word for me, and I could work as a maid at Melbury House as you suggested."

"Perhaps," George replied. "I wish there was a way for all of you to be able to stop working at the brickyard. It's hard for Aunt Maude, and she's not getting any younger. Mrs Webster certainly seemed very taken with you once she got talking."

Penny looked back over her shoulder again, but Abigail Webster had moved away and was deep in conversation with a thickset man in the shadows.

There was something about his face that seemed faintly familiar, and she wondered where she knew him from. He didn't seem like the sort of person Mrs Webster would fraternise with, especially as she seemed determined to rise above her station as a mere coachman's wife.

CHAPTER 7

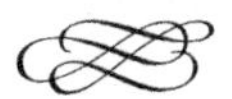

"Put your back into it," Mr Culpepper roared as he stomped towards Penny. "Goodness me, if I was ten years younger, I'd roll up my sleeves and show you what real hard work looks like."

"I'm sorry, sir. I'm going as fast as I can." Penny strained to pick up the handles of her cart and bowed her head against the icy wind. It was late February, and she was still trying to meet her increased quota of bricks that Mr Culpepper had sternly announced on their first day back to work after Christmas. So far, she had only managed by working later into the evenings than ever before, but she was determined not to let Maude down. She knew that Culpepper was itching to throw them out of Willow Cottage and put them in one of the damp tenement buildings down by the docks instead, and she wasn't going to give him the satisfaction. As long as she could meet her daily targets, he would have no cause to take the cottage from them.

"You'll have to finish up by yourself," Culpepper said with a mean glint in his eye. "I don't see why I should have to stay late just because of your laziness. If only Tom was still here. Nell and Jacob are far sturdier than you, Miss Frost. Perhaps you should ask them to show you how to work harder...I expect it's poor breeding that's letting you down," he added with his usual spite.

"As you wish, Mr Culpepper," Penny replied, not rising to his digs about her capabilities.

"Sir...my Billy ain't feeling too good." One of the other workers came hurrying across the yard, pulling her young son with her. The boy doubled over and let off a volley of sneezes which made Mr Culpepper back away in alarm.

"This is most inconvenient, Mrs Dobbs. Billy was meant to be minding the kilns tonight." He pulled out a voluminous handkerchief and covered his mouth as the boy started coughing. Billy's eyes were red and watery, and he looked as though he could barely stand. "I hope it's nothing catching. The last thing we want is some dreadful sickness sweeping through all my workers and leaving me short-handed."

"Have a heart, Mr Culpepper." Penny dropped her barrow and put her hands on her hips. "The poor lad is ill, and all you can think about is the bricks. What about a bit of compassion for the little mite? He's too young to be staying up all night anyway," she added before she could stop herself. "It's not right, he needs his sleep."

"I beg your pardon. How dare you speak to me like that," Culpepper spluttered, glaring at her.

"It ain't no bother usually, Mr Culpepper," Mrs Dobbs said hastily. She shot Penny an apologetic look, knowing that she had only been trying to help.

"I suppose your husband is already partaking of too much ale at the tavern to take the boy's place." Culpepper scowled as he thought about his pleasant evening at home by the fire, enjoying a cigar after a hearty roast dinner being ruined by the inconsiderate way in which his workers kept getting sick.

"Yes, Mr Dobbs said he had some business to

attend to at The Saddlers Arms when he left an hour ago."

"I bet he did," Culpepper grumbled.

"I'd offer myself, but my sister's nippers are ailing, and I promised I'd look after them."

Culpepper glanced around the brickyard, which was now almost deserted, and sighed again. He had promised Sir Henry Calder only last week that production was going well and that they would be ready to supply the last batch of bricks for the orangery in good time. More to the point, Sir Henry had offered him a considerable bonus if the estate's builders could complete the renovations at Talbot Manor early, as his new wife was growing impatient with it all.

"I don't mind staying here for the night to watch the kilns," Penny offered. It was her least favourite job, but she figured it might help her get back in his good books.

A look of relief washed over Mrs Dobbs' face, and she picked her son up, eager to get home as soon as she could.

"Just a moment, Mrs Dobbs." Culpepper held up a bony finger. "I can't afford for Miss Frost to be half asleep tomorrow. As helpful as her suggestion is, I don't want her watching the kilns all night long. Get along to The Saddlers and tell that lazy husband of yours that if he wants to be paid this week, he must come back at midnight and take over from Miss Frost."

Mrs Dobbs nodded hastily. "Of course, Mr Culpepper. He ain't a bad man. A pint of ale is one of his few pleasures, but I'll make sure he's here at the stroke of midnight." She hurried away before he could change his mind. "I'll let Maude know you're minding the kilns and not to expect you home," she called back over her shoulder, shooting Penny a grateful smile.

"As for you, Miss Frost, you needn't think that you can have a late start in the morning just because you're working tonight. I'll expect you here with the rest of your family at six o'clock sharp tomorrow morning, is that understood?"

"Yes, Mr Culpepper." Penny rubbed her hands together to warm her cold, cramped fingers and picked her handcart up again.

"And it goes without saying that if you fall asleep and the fires in the kilns go out, you will be thrown out of this job, and your family will lose their delightful cottage." Culpepper gave her a withering look as he pulled his collar up against a sudden blast of cold air that whistled off the sea.

Penny nodded vigorously. "Yes, sir, I understand. You can rely on me." She shivered as she watched Culpepper striding away. He hadn't even mentioned that Penny would have to do without anything to eat, but it was only what she'd come to expect from the miserly manager.

THE NIGHT WATCH dragged by slowly. Several hours had passed, and Penny picked up her lamp again and trudged across the yard past the hack to complete another round of checks. It was a long, open-sided shed where the wet bricks were laid out to dry, a process which took up to seven weeks at this time of year when the air was cold and wet, which always made Mr Culpepper even more bad-tempered than usual.

Even though she knew the brickyard site like the back of her hand, it felt unfamiliar in the dead of night. She was used to having the background chatter of the other families who worked there to keep her company, but now all she could hear was the thin whine of the wind as it seeped through every nook and cranny. A thick fog had rolled in off the sea since Mr Culpepper had left, which made her feel disorientated. Shadows pressed in on her, and the weak pool of light from her lamp did little to push the thick darkness back.

She hummed one of Tom's sea shanties to try and keep her spirits up as she stumbled past the hack and groped her way towards the beehive-shaped kilns where the dried bricks were being fired.

A loud screech made her stop in her tracks, and her heart pounded in her chest. It sounded almost like a woman screaming. "Who's there?" Her voice sounded feeble and hesitant. "Show yourself," she called a bit louder.

There was another screech, and suddenly she saw a mangy red fox streak across the ground, practically running over her feet. Relief flooded through her, and she gripped her lamp tighter, praying that the fog might lift as suddenly as it had arrived.

"It's just night animals," she muttered to herself, jumping with alarm as she saw another movement out of the corner of her eye. A large grey rat paused from where it was scrabbling through a mound of rubbish behind the shed and gave her a bold stare before slinking away. The sight of its slithering tail and the thought that there were probably dozens more of the creatures made Penny shudder.

A little while later, the muffled sound of the church bells chiming lifted her spirits as she realised Mr Dobbs would be arriving to take over from her in a couple of hours.

Once she was at the kilns, Penny edged her way around them carefully, peering in to check that they were still alight. The fog in that area of the brickyard was filled with a strange orange glow, and she felt the blast of heat from the mixture of faggots, coal, and waste brash from the Talbot Manor estate's woodlands which made up the combustible materials to keep the bricks fired. It would be five long weeks until they would finally be ready to use, and each kiln was at a different stage of the cycle. Doing it that way meant there was always a regular supply of Culpepper's Bricks available to Sir Henry and other discerning customers, as Mr Culpepper liked to tell them often.

A wave of tiredness washed over Penny as she found a sheltered spot near the kilns to rest for a few minutes. She set her lamp on the ground and pulled her cloak tighter to try and keep the dank fog out. The solitude allowed her time to think back to her birthday when George had kissed her, and she brushed the spot on her cheek again as a small smile curved her mouth. Since that day, Penny knew that she had all but given her heart to George. Even though she was still only fourteen, she'd had to grow up fast, like most working girls her age. Her ma had always done her best to educate her with the books at Maude's house, but formal schooling had been a luxury they couldn't afford once Louisa had passed away. Maude needed every penny, so even attending the poor school had been out of the question when there was the chance to start earning a few shillings a week working for Culpepper with the rest of the Bevans.

Nell had turned eighteen several weeks earlier, and Walter, her beau, was already talking about marriage. Penny felt a flutter of excitement in her stomach at the thought that it might be her turn in a few years too. In her imagination, she and George had a quaint cottage with roses growing around the door and two tousle-haired children playing in the garden. She sighed happily, wondering if George had a similar dream. He often spoke about wanting to become the head coachman for Sir Henry, and the way he described it was as though it was perfectly natural that Penny would be part of his future.

Perhaps Sir Henry might have a cottage in his grounds which George would get once Mr Webster retires. The thought filled a pleasant few minutes as Penny rested until she was snapped back to the present at the sound of the muffled chimes of the church clock again.

She stood up hastily and rubbed her chilled, aching limbs. The cold and damp had seeped into her bones, and the fog seemed thicker than ever.

"Penny? Are you there?" A gruff voice drifted towards her, followed by the sound of slow footsteps. There was a sudden clatter, followed by cursing. "Hold yer lamp up, girl. I can't see a thing in this wretched pea-souper. If I trip over and break me neck, the wife won't be very pleased."

"Mr Dobbs, is that you?" Penny's heart beat faster. It was impossible to see which direction he was approaching from. "I'm next to the kilns." She held her lamp up higher and swung it to and fro, hoping that it would guide him the right way.

"There you are." Mr Dobbs loomed out of the murk in front of her and rubbed his eyes blearily with one hand. He smelt of ale, and Penny realised that it wasn't only the fog that was making him unsteady on his feet.

"Are you drunk?" Penny couldn't keep the annoyance out of her voice. If Mr Dobbs wasn't capable of minding the kilns, she would have to stay all night, and she was already feeling exhausted.

"Nothing that a mug of coffee won't sort out." He grinned as he produced a tin mug from behind his back with the other hand. "Mrs Dobbs is like a terrier after a rabbit when she comes to fetch me from the tavern, but she knows I'll be fine as long as I have me coffee." He took a slurp of the thick, strong brew and chuckled at Penny's exasperated expression.

"I'd better wait a little while longer to make sure you're alright," Penny replied. "How's young Billy feeling now?"

The mention of his son seemed to help sober Mr Dobbs up, and he shook his head with a worried frown. "Not so good. I wish he didn't have to work at this rotten place, but we ain't got no choice. It's high time Mr Culpepper raised our wages, but I don't expect he will anytime soon, the old skinflint."

Penny nodded sympathetically. The Dobbs had

already lost two children to scarlet fever, yet Mr Culpepper found it hard to show them any compassion. It was no wonder Mr Dobbs enjoyed a few ales to forget his worries now and again. "We have to keep on hoping that the reformers might persuade parliament to improve our lives one day," Penny said gently. "People tell me that Sir Henry is a kindhearted man. Maybe he doesn't realise that Mr Culpepper treats his workers badly, even though the brickyards are owned by the Calder family."

Mr Dobbs harrumphed. "What do the toffs care? As long as we do their bidding, the wealthy ladies and gents are happy to look the other way." He scratched his chin thoughtfully and then drained the rest of his coffee before tucking the battered mug into his coat pocket. "Perhaps Sir Henry's new wife will make him see sense, not that I know anything about her. It ain't right that us poor folk work until we're fit to drop, and all for barely enough money to make ends meet."

With that observation, he stomped away, leaving Penny wondering whether it was still too soon for her to leave.

"You can go home now, maid," Mr Dobbs added over his shoulder, answering her unasked question. "All this worry about my Billy has sobered me up now. I'll be fine here by myself. You'd better get a few hours of sleep, otherwise Maude will have my guts for garters."

Penny smiled to herself as she picked up her lamp. Mr Dobbs was a kindly man under his gruff exterior, and she hoped Billy would be feeling better soon.

"Don't forget to leave your lamp by Culpepper's office," Mr Dobbs called from the gloom which had already engulfed him. "You know it will be the first thing he'll check. Goodnight, maid. See you tomorrow."

PENNY SHIVERED and glanced along the street a few minutes later. The snow was still thick on the ground, and the sulphurous glow of the gas lamps was barely enough to light her route back to the cottage. It was long past midnight, and she felt a sense of unease at how silent the streets were. The weather had sent even the hardiest drinkers home from the pubs earlier than usual, and the street urchins had long since scurried away to find whatever shelter they could. The familiar landmarks which marked the route she took home every day seemed distorted and somehow menacing as tendrils of fog drifted across the town like ghostly wraiths. Penny had always had an active imagination, and goosebumps tingled on her arms as she recalled the ghost stories that Tom used to tell them by the fire on a winter's night.

"Just a few more streets to go, and then I'll be home safe and sound," she muttered under her breath. The tantalising thought of a hot cup of tea and a slice of bread and jam made her stomach growl with hunger, and she quickened her pace. No doubt Maude would have left something out for her, as well as a candle burning in the window.

Suddenly Penny felt a sense of foreboding as she saw the dark entrance of an alleyway ahead. There was something about the impenetrable shadows that reminded her of the night she had been attacked by the pickpockets.

"Come on, Penny, don't be silly," she whispered, trying to keep her imagination in check. "That turned out to be a blessing in disguise because it's when George came to my rescue." Penny lifted her chin and walked faster, telling herself that there was nothing to fear.

The steady rumble of a cart trundling through the snow behind her made her shake off her fanciful imaginings, and she chuckled at the thought of telling George about it the following evening after work. He always came to eat at Willow Cottage with the family on Tuesdays, and she couldn't wait to see him again.

"Evening, miss." The man sitting at the front of the cart lifted his hand in a greeting and pulled on the reins to stop the stocky pony that was pulling it. "Terrible weather, ain't it." His greasy cap was pulled low, and he had a scarf wrapped around the bottom of his face so that all that showed were his eyes.

"It'll blow over in the morning, I'm sure." Penny glanced in the back of the cart, which was full of rags, wondering what the fellow was doing abroad at such a late hour. Was he working late or starting early? Either way, he would get no trade in the middle of the night.

"Work never ends for a rag-and-bone man," he said as if reading her thoughts. "Per'aps you've got something to give me? Live around here, do you?"

Penny shook her head and pointed at the entrance to the courtyard up ahead. "I'm almost home now, and no, I'm sorry, we always save our rubbish to give to old Mr Flinty. He's the regular rag and bone man who usually works these streets."

Suddenly there was movement in the rags, and a second man jumped lightly down from the back of the cart. He was at Penny's side in three long strides. "Well, that ain't very charitable, is it, Miss Frost?" he sneered.

"Wh...what? How do you know my name?" Penny stumbled backwards as his cold gaze bored into her. His face was covered, just like the driver's, and she had no idea who he was.

"That's none of your concern." He stepped closer again, and Penny looked wildly around for help.

"I must go now...George is expecting me home any minute. In fact, he's probably about to come around the corner right now to look for me." She took a deep breath to scream, but before she could utter another word, the man sprang forward and threw a blanket over her head.

"Let...me...go..." Penny tried to wriggle free, but it was futile. The man's arms were clamped around her like a vice, and he bundled her roughly into the back of the cart.

"I'm sure George is fast asleep, without a care

in the world." The man sniggered quietly. "On we go, driver. Time for us to make ourselves scarce."

The cart jerked forward as the pony trotted on, and Penny blinked back the tears that pricked at the back of her eyes. *I have to stay calm...they know me...there must be a reason this is happening...* The thoughts pounded through her mind, and she prayed that somehow George and Turk would come to save her again, just like they had all those years before.

CHAPTER 8

A thin shaft of grey daylight filtered through the grimy window as Penny's eyes fluttered open, and she dazedly took in her unfamiliar surrounding. For a second, she wondered whether she had fallen asleep at the brickyard and the breath caught in her throat at the thought of Mr Culpepper's anger when he discovered her misdemeanour. But the rickety chair and table in the corner of the room looked nothing like his office, and the noise of clanking from outside sounded all wrong.

She tried to sit up and winced as pain shot through the muscles of her shoulders. Her hands were bound tightly behind her back, and her head throbbed, making her feel groggy.

"Help!" Penny coughed as the word stuck in her throat. It had come out as barely more than a whisper, and she groaned as the memories from the night before came flooding back.

She recalled that the cart ride hadn't seemed to last very long, which meant that the men had probably taken her somewhere within the town of Brynwell. It was something small to be grateful for. When they had come to a stop, she had been dragged unceremoniously off the cart and thrown over one of their shoulders. They had clomped up some stairs and dumped her straight onto what felt like a thin, lumpy mattress on the floor.

When the blanket had been removed, she had still been none the wiser about who had abducted her. Their faces were still covered, except for their eyes, and there was only one stubby candle flickering on the table.

"Who are you, and what do you want with me?" she had managed to gasp as they forced her hands behind her back and swiftly tied them. The rope had dug cruelly into her slim wrists, but when she told them, they just grunted and shrugged.

"Drink this and keep quiet, or else." The man who had driven the cart produced a hip flask and held it to Penny's lips.

At first, she had refused, pressing her lips tightly together until she saw him raise his fist.

"It's the drink or a clout around the head. Your choice," he muttered. The other man had paced back and forth, clearly worried that things might escalate.

"Ain't nobody around to hear you, so there's no point calling for help," he said, suddenly stopping in front of her and bending over to examine her as though she was a curiosity. "Do as you're told, and everything will go a lot easier for you, Miss Frost."

The bitter liquid made Penny's eyes water as she gulped it down. It was wine, but there was something else in it too, which left a strange taste in her mouth.

"Please tell me…" The last thing Penny remembered as she drifted into a deep sleep was the door slamming shut and the sound of a key turning to lock her in.

The rhythmical sound of clanking outside brought her back to the present again, and she tipped her head to one side, trying to place what it could be. It reminded her of the time Tom had taken them all down to the harbour to show them a ship similar to the clipper he would be working on.

"It's rigging on the ships," she mumbled after listening for a moment longer. It wasn't muffled, which must mean that the fog had lifted and she was somewhere near the docks. Taking a deep breath, she managed to scramble to her feet. Her head swam, and for one sickening moment, she thought she was going to faint, but gradually, her vision cleared, and she felt the strength returning to her limbs, fueled by anger and determination.

"They can't do this to me," she said firmly. She looked around to see if there was some way she might be able to escape. The first thing she needed to do was get the rope off her wrists, and then she would be able to see if she could prise the window open. She stumbled over to the chair and sat down for a second to gather her energy. The effects of the laudanum in the wine had worn off at long last, and the groggy feeling receded, leaving her clear-headed as she surveyed the room.

At first glance, there was nothing more than the thin mattress, a small table, and the chair she was sitting on. But then she noticed that the brick fireplace surround sat proud from the wall. There was no fire lit in the hearth, and the room was perishing cold, but Penny didn't care about that. What mattered was the fact that the rough edge of the hearth was accessible to her. She crossed the room quickly and stood with her back to it, rasping the rope against the edge of the bricks that were supporting the mantel shelf. Her breath plumed around her head, but the vigorous movement soon warmed her up. She frowned with concentration, determined to take her safety into her own hands, and after what felt like an age, she finally felt the tight tension around her wrists release as the strands of the rope unravelled.

"That'll teach you to underestimate me," Penny muttered with a grim smile of satisfaction. She rubbed her wrist and hands and winced as her circulation was restored before dragging the chair to the window.

Her optimism was short-lived. The window catch had rusted closed with disuse, and when she spat on the corner of her apron to clean the glass, she realised that she was several storeys up in what appeared to be some sort of old warehouse. Even if she could break the glass and wriggle through without cutting herself, there were no other rooftops nearby that she could crawl out onto. It was a sheer drop outside the window, and she risked broken bones and possibly worse if she fell from that height.

Not to be deterred, Penny turned her attention to the door. It was made from sturdy wood on heavy hinges, and there wasn't even a knothole or a chink between the planks that she could peek through as the damp air had made the wood swell. She twisted the handle cautiously. For all she knew, her abductors could be keeping guard outside. The doorknob yielded to her touch without so much as a squeak, but when she tugged, the door didn't budge. She was locked in.

She could feel panic starting to rise in her chest as she knelt down to look through the keyhole. But even that had been stuffed with a rag, so there was nothing to see.

What will become of me? Penny walked around the room in an attempt to calm her racing thoughts. Ten small steps each way…like a prison cell that she had once heard one of the women at the brickyard describe from visiting her husband in the clink. *Will I ever see dear George...and Maude and Nell and Jacob again?* Tears pooled in her eyes as she realised with a shock that by now, they would know she was missing.

She could almost picture Maude's furrowed brow as she demanded answers from Mr Culpepper and his airy dismissal of her worries as he took the chance to tell Maude how unreliable she was for not showing up to work. George was probably running through the streets of Brynwell right that very minute, stopping every passer-by to ask if they had seen a dark-haired girl walking home in the middle of the night.

But Penny remembered that the streets had been deserted. Nobody had heard her shout for help or witnessed her being bundled into the cart. She was completely alone in the world, with no way of escaping.

At this realisation, Penny sat back down heavily on the chair and wept.

"If only I'd stayed at the kilns with Mr Dobbs," she whispered, pressing her apron over her eyes to mop up the tears. She would have given anything to be lugging bricks across the yard like a normal day; it was hard work but wonderfully safe compared to her perilous situation. And the memory of all the times she had longed for a better life seemed to mock her as she yearned for her cosy bedroom under the eaves and the sound of Maude and Nell's chatter drifting up the stairs.

What if they think I've run away? The thought made Penny gasp out loud. She couldn't bear the idea that George might think she'd left. He had always chuckled when she talked wistfully of having more money one day, saying that he was more than content with what they had…and now he might be wondering if she had left him behind, lured by the fanciful notion of a more exciting future somewhere else.

"Why couldn't I have been happy with everything just the way it was? If only I'd realised how lucky I was to have the things that really mattered." Penny jumped as a pigeon landed on the windowsill and eyed her beadily through the glass, hoping for some crumbs.

She sighed and then shook her head. "I don't have anything to give you." The bird pecked at the glass and then puffed its chest out to coo loudly. A moment later, another pigeon arrived with a clatter of wings, making Penny smile. It was a bit of company, which was all she needed to remind herself that all was not lost. She had to believe that she would find a way out of this terrible situation because the alternative was unthinkable. Someone was bound to walk past the warehouse sooner or later, so she would bang on the window and be reunited with George and the others in no time.

. . .

While the pigeons kept Penny entertained, the grey light gradually brightened until she even spotted a patch of blue sky above the rooftops. It was turning out to be a crisp winter's day, the sort that made a person think that spring wasn't far away.

Suddenly the sound of heavy footsteps on the stairs drifted through the door, and Penny's heart sank as she heard a key in the lock. The handle turned, and the door swung open to reveal the two men who were the cause of all her woes.

"Don't come near me." Penny grabbed the chair and held it in front of her for protection. There was no point in pretending her hands were still bound.

One of the men chuckled. "What do you think you are? A lion tamer?" He sauntered closer and took hold of the chair, twisting it out of her grasp and setting it back down next to the table.

"Water and some bread and jam." The other man plonked a basket on the table and then slammed the door shut behind them. "We thought you'd be hungry and thirsty. Unless you'd rather we took it away again?"

Penny's stomach growled at the sight of the food, and she shook her head. It was only now that she realised how thirsty she was as well. "Is it just water, or have you put laudanum in it again?" she demanded.

"Ach, stop yer fussing. You had a good night's sleep, didn't you? It was only a couple of drops to stop you shouting for help while we sorted out a few things."

The men removed their scarves and looked at each other, and Penny felt a shiver of déja vu. "Neville? And Alf? You're the two boys who tried to steal my money in the alleyway when I was a nipper. I thought there was something familiar about you when I saw you last night."

"We've got a proper little bright spark here, Alf," Neville said, grinning at his brother. He folded his arms and nodded. "You've got a good memory, Miss Frost, I'll give you that. It must be what…almost six years ago."

"Just over six years ago," Penny said sharply. "I never forget someone who wants to do me wrong."

"Well, it's almost like we're old acquaintances then. All the more reason to do what we say." Alf smirked and picked up the remains of the frayed rope between his fingers before throwing it into the empty fireplace. "Don't try any more tricks like that, and we'll get along just fine."

Penny gave them both a smile, even though it pained her to do so. She needed them to think that she was biddable just for long enough to make them get careless so she could escape. "I don't suppose you'd care to tell me why you've kidnapped me?" she asked lightly. "It's not as if a girl who works at Culpepper's Brickyard is worth a great deal to two fine gentlemen like you. You've come up in the world since you were pickpockets."

Neville shot her a suspicious look, wondering whether she was being rude, but Alf puffed his chest out, happy to take the compliment.

"Some folks might look down on us for having a rag and bone business, but it pays alright," Neville muttered. "It's just been the two of us for as long as we can remember, but we managed to get away from that awful gang."

"And that's all credit to you." Penny felt a moment of grudging admiration for them in spite of herself. She knew better than anyone how hard it was to survive if you didn't have a family to look out for you. "So…why am I here?" she prompted again.

"You'll find out soon enough." Alf looked shifty. "We're just the messengers, if you get my drift. So we're not at liberty to tell you anything else at the moment."

"You mean you're the monkey, not the organ grinder?" Penny shot back. She regretted it as Alf's expression darkened.

"Don't think you can get around us by being friendly," he growled. "You always were a hoity-toity miss. George ain't going to come to your rescue with that ugly old dog of his this time, so you'd better watch yer manners."

"I'm sorry, it's all been a bit of a shock." Penny pulled the basket over and took out the bread and jam. There were several slices, which surprised her. "Would you like to share this with me?" she asked as Neville watched her.

"We better hadn't. You probably need it more than us. Besides, if everything goes to plan, we'll have enough money for a hot dinner every day for the rest of the year by nightfall."

The bread was fresh, and the room fell silent as Penny ate it as quickly as was polite, washing it down with the water, which tasted slightly musty. There was no telling when she might be fed again, and she had been feeling light-headed with hunger. It was hard to believe that the last time she had eaten was a wedge of cold pie for lunch with

Maude at the brickyard the previous day. The thought made her feel sad again, and she blinked hastily. She didn't want Neville and Alf to see her cry.

Neville's cryptic comment about the money niggled away at her while she chewed the bread. It made no sense to her at all, but he didn't seem to be joking. In one way, it gave her hope. For some reason, she was valuable to them, which meant that they would treat her well. She cast her mind over what they might have planned for her but then wished she hadn't. Her blood ran cold as she remembered Sal telling her about young women who were forced to become ladies of ill repute to earn money for their pimps. Even the high-class ones who were treated lavishly in high-class brothels were still forced to do things against their will for the toffs who would pay handsomely, not that they ever got the keep the money for themselves.

A memory of George's warm brown eyes came to Penny and the way he treated her with such kindness and courtesy. If Neville and Alf were planning to make her become a lady of the night, George would never want to see her again.

I have to escape now before it's too late. The

thought slid into her mind, and she was fired up with a new sense of resolve. They hadn't locked the door, which meant this was her only opportunity.

"Could I ask you to do one small thing for me, please?" Penny gave them a sweet smile, hoping that they wouldn't notice the tremor of fear in her voice.

"You can ask, but it ain't necessarily something we'll agree to," Neville said with a chuckle. His good humour was restored at the thought of all the money coming his way, and he was already thinking about how they might be able to buy a second pony and cart and expand the business, as well as get better lodgings.

"I'm still feeling a bit groggy from the effects of the laudanum last night. Could you open the window for me? Just so I can get some fresh air while you're here."

Alf glanced at Neville, who nodded. "I assume you've seen you can't get out that way, so I suppose it won't harm." The pigeons clattered away as Alf grappled with the rusty catch. "Looks like it ain't been opened for years. Give me a hand, Neville, don't just stand there."

Neville joined his brother and scratched his

head as they looked at the window. As quick as a flash, as soon as they had their backs to her, Penny jumped up, picked up her skirts, and darted to the door, wrenching it open.

"Come back, you slippery wench." Neville's shout echoed in the stairwell as he dived after her, with Alf two steps behind.

"Don't let her get away," Alf bellowed. "She'll have the constable on us in no time."

Penny stumbled down the stairs. There were no windows, and some of the steps felt rotten under her feet. As much as she wanted to run as fast as she could, she knew she had to take care otherwise, she might end up in a crumpled heap at the bottom.

Neville and Alf had the advantage of knowing the layout of the stairs better than she did, and their heavy footsteps were getting closer and closer behind her. In one last act of desperation, Penny leapt down the last few steps and sprinted towards the outer door, practically sobbing at the thought of being outside and free again.

As she reached for the handle, the door suddenly flew open, and she ran headlong into the chest of a tall man, who gripped her tightly around her arms. She looked up and gasped as she recognised him.

"Mr Webster...thank goodness it's you..." She could hardly speak for the sense of relief that crashed over her. Help had come after all.

"These dreadful men kidnapped me on my way home last night...thew me in their cart...and drugged me and held me captive until this morning...they won't say why but I can only think the worst...please...send for the constable...they mustn't be allowed to get away with it...and I need to tell George I'm safe...he'll be going out of his mind with worry." Penny's words came out in ragged gasps as she explained what had happened.

"Goodness me, my dear. There's no need to make such a scene. You're perfectly safe." Abigail Webster tutted as she peered around her husband's portly frame and looked Penny up and down.

"But you don't understand...they kidnapped me and held me captive," Penny cried. She wondered why the woman wasn't hurrying away to call for the constable already.

"I wouldn't describe it quite like that," Abigail continued, waving her handkerchief as though Penny was being ridiculous. "They were merely looking after you until it was safe for Percival and me to come and have a little chat with you about our plan."

Penny felt the ground tilt beneath her feet, and if it hadn't been for Mr Webster's hands around her arms, she would have keeled over. "You...you mean you knew about this?" she croaked.

"Of course, dear," Abigail trilled, giving her husband a happy smile. She gestured at Neville and Alf with a look of amusement. "You don't think these two ruffians came up with the idea, do you? No, no, no...this is all down to us."

CHAPTER 9

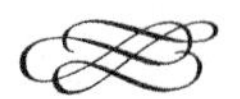

Penny could scarcely believe what Abigail Webster was saying, but as she saw Neville nodding rather apologetically, she knew it must be true.

"We didn't mean to scare you, Miss Frost," Alf muttered. "But we couldn't risk you getting away until the Websters spoke to you." He scuffed his boot on the floor. "That's why we gave you the laudanum, so you wouldn't panic."

"The money we've been promised for doing this will make all the difference to our business," Neville added gruffly. "It's hard to get ahead when you've been brought up on the streets like we were."

"I suppose I can forgive you," Penny said, giving

them both an exasperated look. "But I would like an explanation, Mr Webster. You, of all people, must know how worried George will be."

Percy Webster shot a guilty look at his wife, which made Penny think the kidnapping must be more Abigail's idea than his. "I'll let my dear wife explain," he said, ushering Abigail into the gloomy hallway.

Abigail seemed only too happy to take all the credit. "It's quite the most wonderful thing, Penny. When you hear what I have to say, you'll see that last night was just a minor inconvenience compared to how much better life is about to become for you."

"I'm not sure I understand." Penny was still finding it hard to accept that the Websters were involved, and it felt as though everyone was talking in riddles. "I'm happy living at Maude's... even working at Culpepper's Brickworks, although I had hoped you might be able to put in a good word for me if there was a chance to work as a maid at Melbury House. George said it would be better than lugging bricks, and we could see more of each other, what with him working in the stables..." She blushed as Neville and Alf nudged each other. "We're not courting if that's what you think, but he's my best friend."

"None of that is relevant," Abigail interjected. "I'm not interested in your fanciful notions of romance. There's something far more important at stake here."

Penny folded her arms and sighed. "Well, why don't you just tell me then? I'm still not happy about being kidnapped, and I'm sure the constable wouldn't be either."

"A bit of politeness wouldn't go amiss." Mr Webster jerked his head, and Neville hurried to block the doorway with his burly frame. There was no way Penny was going to be allowed to escape again, and her shoulders sagged as she accepted that she was still at their mercy.

Abigail drew herself up to her full height and launched into the explanation that Penny was craving. "When we saw you and George ice skating at the river before Christmas, I was most intrigued by your brooch, as you know."

Penny instantly felt defensive. The brooch was her most treasured possession and her only link to her dear mama, and it felt somehow distasteful to be discussing it in the filthy warehouse with strangers. "I don't have it on me now if you're thinking of stealing it," she said stiffly.

"What do you take me for?" Abigail sniffed and looked offended. "Hear me out, will you? It was the mother-of-pearl dove on the brooch which caught my eye. It reminded me of something, and a couple of days later, I remembered what it was."

Neville and Alf listened attentively. Clearly, it was the first time they had heard Abigail's explanation as well.

"I thought it was just a pretty brooch," Penny said. "Its only value is to me, surely, because it was my ma's. Maude is as honest as they come, by the way. She could have sold it when I was still a nipper, and I would never have known, but she kept it safe for me, just like Ma asked her to."

"Thank goodness she did." Abigail's eyes gleamed with intrigue. "The little dove on your brooch is the same likeness as a dove which is on the Calder family's coat of arms, you see. I saw the coat of arms once when Sir Henry had a garden party at Talbot Manor for his best workers. Very grand it was too. Which is why I think your brooch is rather important, especially how it came to be in your mother's possession."

Penny bristled with indignation. "She wasn't a

thief if that's what you're implying. My ma would never have stolen it." She thought back to how Louisa had never even mentioned the brooch to her while she was still alive. It had been tucked away like some sort of secret, and even when she had given it to Maude for safekeeping, it had remained shrouded in mystery.

"My wife is not saying that your ma was a common thief, Miss Frost." Percy nodded for Abigail to continue with the story.

"Quite the opposite, in fact," Abigail said with a tremor of excitement in her voice. "We are convinced that you are Sir Henry's granddaughter, Penny. His daughter, Louisa, disappeared without a trace many years ago, and there were always rumours of some sort of scandal about it. But given that you have a remarkable likeness to Sir Henry…and the fact that your ma gave you the brooch…we think you are part of the Calder family."

Penny's mouth gaped open as she tried to take in what Abigail Webster had just told her. "Are you sure? It seems unbelievable." She felt a ripple of emotion run through her. "If it's true, I must tell Maude," she muttered. Her mind was whirling at the implications of these revelations. "She will want to accompany me to meet Sir Henry…and George will as well." Laughter suddenly bubbled up in her chest. "To think, George has been working for Sir Henry in his stables at Melbury House for all these years, and we never realised. Maybe Sir Henry will be able to promote him to a better paid position…and Maude might be able to stop work at Mr Culpeppers. I've heard that Sir Henry is kindhearted, so I'm sure he'll want to thank the Bevans for raising me—"

Abigail held up her hand, stopping the flow of Penny's eager chatter. "Just a moment. I must insist that you have to let me and Mr Webster conduct your introduction. If it's left to Maude, it will go horribly wrong, I'm sure. I know her of old, and she doesn't have a genteel bone in her body. Sir Henry will probably think you're a couple of chancers."

"That's no way to talk about Maude," Penny said hotly. She was suddenly filled with doubt and suspicion again. "Now I come to think about it, why exactly are you being so helpful all of a sudden? You could have just told me about Sir Henry's coat of arms weeks ago and let me decide what to do next."

"It's out of the goodness of our hearts, of

course," Abigail replied soothingly. There was a flash of irritation in her eyes, and then she summoned a smile again. "You don't understand how well-to-do folk like to do things, my dear, what with being a lowly worker at the brickyards. It's not Maude's fault, but she would only mess things up; bless her. Mr Webster has worked for Sir Henry for years, and we know what's best in this situation."

"What's best?" Penny sounded doubtful and wished she could speak to George. She still wasn't sure whether the Websters could be trusted. "You got these two to kidnap me, and you seem very keen not to let me speak to my adopted family…or the constable, for that matter."

"I know this has all come as a great surprise, but we only have your best interests at heart." Abigail sounded as though she was starting to lose patience with Penny's comments, and Mr Webster pulled his pocket watch out and tutted.

"Time is getting on, my dear. We may as well tell her the rest."

"Oh, alright." Abigail glared at Neville and Alf. "This isn't to be repeated, is that clear? You'll get the money we agreed, and that's it."

The two men nodded enthusiastically. "Yes,

Mrs Webster. We won't repeat it to a soul…as long as you honour your side of the bargain." Neville smiled and flexed his broad shoulders, making his intentions clear.

"We've made some enquiries, and a few years ago, it appears that Sir Henry was willing to offer a reward for information about where his daughter, Louisa, went."

"So it comes down to money, does it?" Now it was all starting to make sense to Penny. "You want to take me to meet Sir Henry, so you get some sort of financial reward."

"Well, if it wasn't for my quick thinking, you'd still be lugging bricks for Mr Culpepper." Abigail gave a self-righteous huff of annoyance. "Why shouldn't we be rewarded for reuniting you with your true family? Any money is rightfully ours, which is why I don't want Maude Bevan sticking her nose in and interfering. Percy and I have worked hard for the family all these years, so I ain't letting this opportunity slip out of our hands, missy, no matter what you say."

Alf stifled a chuckle as Abigail's carefully cultured veneer of respectability cracked to show her humble beginnings. "You ain't so different from the rest of us then, Mrs Webster. Anything to make a bit more money, eh?"

"Don't be so impertinent." Abigail recovered her composure and hurried over to stand by Penny's side. "Returning Penny to the bosom of her proper family will make Sir Henry very happy, and the money he gives us will be a trifle in comparison to the joy he will gain."

"We'd better get a move on," Mr Webster said, reminding everyone that there was still work to do.

"The first thing is to get you a better gown, my dear. We don't want you meeting your grandpapa looking like you've spent the night on the streets, or smelling of mouse droppings, do we."

Abigail was all smiles again, and Penny decided it was best not to remind her that she had spent the night drugged with laudanum and trussed up like a Christmas turkey. "I have a nicer dress which I wear for Sunday best," she said hesitantly. Now that she had got over her shock, she was starting to look forward to meeting Sir Henry.

"Oh, no, that won't do at all. We're going to the second-hand clothes shop to get you something a little more presentable." Abigail tucked Penny's hand into the crook of her arm and swept her back outside into the bright winter sunshine. "We want you to look clean and tidy but not too well off, so Sir Henry realises what a difficult start you've had in life. Saving his little waif of a granddaughter from a life of hardship is going to make him forever indebted towards me and Mr Webster," she added happily.

AN HOUR LATER, Penny did a twirl in front of the tall mirror in Mrs Zachariah's second-hand clothes shop as Abigail looked on. The green gown was plain but showed off her chestnut curls nicely, and more importantly, Penny didn't have to pay for it. The lace collar was slightly yellowed with age, and the cut was old-fashioned, but she didn't mind in the slightest. Having something new was a rare treat.

"Maude always says I suit green," Penny said happily to Mrs Zachariah, who was darting around her, making small adjustments, so the gown sat perfectly over Penny's curves.

"Tell her I have plenty more where this came from, duckie. A dress for every occasion and every budget, I always say to my customers."

A sudden pang of homesickness gripped Penny

as she realised that she wouldn't be chattering about her good fortune over a cup of tea with Nell and Maude later that evening. Instead, she would be meeting her new family. She came to a sudden decision, which she knew Mrs Webster might not like, but she had to do, regardless.

"We have to go to Willow Cottage before we do anything else," Penny said firmly to Abigail as they left the shop. "It's not fair on Maude and the others to just send a message through Neville that I'm alright. I know that's the way you want to do it, but my conscience won't allow it. Maude is like a second mother to me, and I love Nell and Jacob... and George is my best friend. They will want to know my news."

Abigail's lips pinched together in a disapproving line. It was a look Penny was coming to recognise, that she liked to get her own way. "I think it's better to introduce you to Sir Henry first. Maude won't be able to resist claiming some of the glory for herself. Now hurry up and get back in the carriage."

Mr Webster was waiting patiently with one of the more modest carriages belonging to Melbury House on the side of the street, and Penny knew that if she didn't put her foot down on this one small thing, they would whisk her away and ignore her wishes.

She stopped in her tracks, and a costermonger muttered as he almost crashed into her. "If you don't take me to Willow Cottage, I won't come with you, Mrs Webster." She lifted her chin and gave the woman a defiant look. "Without me, you won't get your money. Maude is a caring, kind-hearted woman, and she'll be worried sick about where I am."

"Oh, very well." Abigail knew when she was beaten. She nodded to Percy as he held the carriage door open. "Take us to Sketty Lane first. We'd better put Maude's mind at rest otherwise, we'll never hear the end of it."

As they settled back against the leather squabs, Penny felt another flutter of anticipation. Usually, she walked everywhere. A carriage ride was a luxury they couldn't afford, but Mrs Webster had already told her that this was one of the old carriages that Sir Henry allowed Mr Webster to use for his own leisure as it was too scruffy for the Calder family now. It seemed in perfectly good condition to her, which only served to show that the wealthy classes had very different standards.

"We may as well use your visit to Willow

Cottage as a chance to get the brooch off Maude," Abigail said thoughtfully. "I'm sure Sir Henry won't doubt who you are when he sees you, but it will help quash any worries he might have if you can show him the brooch as well and explain that it belonged to your mama."

"Ma wanted Maude to look after it for me until I'm eighteen." Penny watched the scruffy street urchins begging for coins at the side of the street, thinking how she could have ended up like them if Maude hadn't taken Louisa in.

"It's not up to Maude anymore," Abigail said firmly. "You have to remember that you're a Calder now, not one of Mrs Bevan's charitable cases. We'll take the brooch, and she'll have to do as I say."

As Mr Webster pulled the glossy horse to a halt on Sketty Lane, the door of Willow Cottage flew open, and Maude came running towards the carriage, with George right behind. Her kindly face was etched with worry, and Penny felt wretched for causing her so much distress.

"Mr Webster…thank goodness you're here," George cried. "Have you heard that Penny has disappeared? We've been looking everywhere…I mean, I fed the horses first, of course, but as soon as my jobs were done, I came straight here to help

Maude look for Penny. Nobody's seen hide nor hair of her." George's voice was hoarse from the last couple of hours of shouting out Penny's name on the streets of Brynwell.

"Don't worry, Mrs Bevan, she's right here in the carriage," Mr Webster said hastily. He sounded slightly guilty, but Penny noticed that Abigail showed no such emotion. If anything, she looked annoyed by Maude's sob of relief as she stepped out of the carriage ahead of Penny.

"Penny, my girl! Where have you been?" Maude folded her into a warm embrace, her plump cheeks flushed with relief. "Mr Dobbs told us you left the brickyards in the early hours of the morning, and nobody's seen you since. Did you have a bump to the head on your way home or something?"

"I…it's hard to explain," Penny began.

"Just wait until I see Mr Culpepper again." Maude looked indignant as she led Penny into the cottage, eying her up for injuries. "It ain't right making a slip of a girl walk home all alone in the snow and fog."

As soon as everyone was back in the kitchen, Maude hastily assembled the teacups and set the kettle to boil on the range. "You need a nice cup of tea and then—" Her words petered out as she realised that Penny was wearing a new dress.

"Have you got a fancy man?" Nell asked, fingering the green gown.

Penny's cheeks turned a fiery red, and she glanced at George, who was studiously avoiding her gaze. His expression was hard to read, and her heart sank. She had imagined being swept into his embrace as part of the reunion, but then she remembered that nobody knew about the kiss they had had on her birthday. "Of course not, Nell, don't be silly." She glanced at George again and thought she detected a look of relief.

"Why don't you let the poor girl get a word in edgeways," George said goodnaturedly, pulling a chair out for Penny to sit at the table. "You look exhausted, Penny. Maybe you'd rather tell us later," he added quietly. His fingers brushed over Penny's hand, and their eyes met for a moment. She could see the confusion behind his kind expression, and suddenly she was overcome with doubt. Everything had felt simple in the carriage...she would tell them about Abigail's discovery, and Sir Henry would welcome all of them. But now she wasn't so sure.

"If you would kindly allow me to explain,"

Abigail said pompously. She looked around the homely, cluttered room, taking in the furniture which had seen better days and shuddered slightly, which made Penny feel disloyal to Maude. She loved Willow Cottage because it held some of her happiest memories.

"Spit it out then, Abigail," Maude said, passing her a cup of tea. "Culpepper will be expecting us to get back to work. It was hard enough persuading him to let us take a couple of hours off to look for Penny as it is." She realised that her old acquaintance still had ideas above her station and thought she was better than the other families who lived in Sketty Lane.

"When you took Louisa in, did you ever know her surname?" Abigail asked, giving Maude a hard stare.

The question took her aback. "The poor woman was in the midst of having a baby. It wasn't the first thing that came to mind."

"But she never revealed who she was, is that correct?"

Maude took a sip of tea, pausing to think for a moment. Her eyes narrowed as she sized Abigail Webster up and wondered what the woman was up to. "She was always just Louisa to us. She never recovered her memory after having a bump on her head the night I found her. What of it? She needed a place to call home, and since my Fred died, we appreciated the company. She was always frail, but she was a good ma to Penny and paid her way with a bit of mending and dressmaking."

"And Penny tells me that the only thing her ma had on her when she arrived was a silver brooch." Abigail seemed uninterested in finding out what Louisa had really been like.

"And she had one penny coin," Nell added. "That's why Penny has that name. Plus, it was a cold night…so we called her Penny Frost. But what business is it of yours?"

"Penny is Sir Henry Calder's long-lost granddaughter, and Mr Webster and I are taking her there now to return her to her rightful family, where she belongs."

There was a moment of stunned silence, and then Nell leapt up. "What a ridiculous idea. Are you saying Louisa was Sir Henry's daughter? What proof do you have." She looked wildly around the room. "Say something, George. Ma? It can't be true, can it? Does that mean Penny will be taken away from our family?"

Maude's cheeks turned pink again, and she

placed a gentle hand on Penny's shoulder. "Hush, Nell. There's no need to get upset."

"Is it really true?" George said, sinking heavily into the chair next to Penny. "Your real name is Penny Calder?" His expression was at once incredulous but also worried. "Are you sure Mrs Webster isn't trying to…raise your hopes falsely?" he whispered.

"The brooch is all the evidence we need," Abigail said grandly. "Plus, Penny herself. I've seen paintings of Sir Henry and his late wife at Talbot Manor, and the likeness is uncanny. I trust you won't stand in her way, Maude? The girl deserves to be reunited with her proper family. And while we're at it, I'd better take the brooch with us. We're leaving immediately."

"I always suspected that Louisa came from a well-educated family, even though she was in rags the night I found her," Maude said slowly. "But I never imagined she was so well-to-do. She never had airs and graces…she was just grateful we took her in." Her eyes misted over for a moment.

"Is this what you want, Penny?" George asked the question which was on everyone's mind. "I mean…that's a silly thing for me to say. Of course, you would want to live at Talbot Manor with your grandfather. It's everything you've ever dreamt of." He smiled, but there was a shadow of sadness in his eyes.

"We must pack your things," Maude said. "It's a wonderful turn of events, my sweet, and if Abigail thought we would stand in your way, then she clearly doesn't know us at all. Your destiny is to be part of the Calder family, and we couldn't be happier for you, Penny."

The next few minutes were a flurry of activity as Maude and Nell rushed around the small cottage, gathering Penny's few possessions and putting them into an old carpetbag.

"She won't need any clothes," Abigail said, mindful of the time passing. "Just the brooch and a few trinkets to remember you by. I'm sure Sir Henry will want her to have a whole new wardrobe of dresses, as will be fitting for her new place in society."

All too soon, Penny was being hurried back out to the carriage by Abigail.

"Wait. I want to say goodbye properly." Penny hung back, suddenly feeling torn again.

"You surely don't want Sir Henry to spend another moment feeling sad about losing his daughter, do you?" Abigail said, sighing impatiently.

"Don't worry, I'm sure we'll still see plenty of you," Maude said. She embraced Penny and then pressed a handkerchief to her cheeks to dab away the tears which were rolling down her wrinkled cheeks.

"Wait until Mr Culpepper finds out who you really are," Nell said with a chuckle. "Perhaps he'll treat us a bit better now, as well."

"I'll speak to Sir Henry, I promise," Penny said hastily. "Maybe I can persuade him to find you a better job."

The horse in front of the carriage fidgeted in the traces, eager to be on its way, and Mr Webster helped Abigail up the steps and then beckoned for Penny to follow.

"We'll still be friends, won't we, George?" Penny gave him a lingering look. "I won't forget about you..."

George leaned forward and brushed a kiss on her cheek. "Of course we will. You're my best friend, Penny, and always have been. Where would I be without you?"

As the carriage rolled away, Penny pressed her face to the window, wanting to watch the people she loved until the last possible moment. Maude's handkerchief fluttered as she waved goodbye, and George held up his hand just as the carriage turned the corner at the end of Sketty Lane.

"Don't think about them," Abigail said crisply. "That's all in the past now. You have a whole new life to look forward to and me to thank for it."

Penny sat back against the squabs and nodded, fighting back her tears. She might be about to go up in the world, but her heart ached for George and everyone else she was leaving behind.

CHAPTER 10

"Are we going to Melbury House to meet Sir Henry?" Penny asked as the carriage rounded the corner. Even though everyone had talked a lot about Talbot Manor, she had a sudden hope that he might prefer to live at the townhouse instead, which would mean she could still see George.

Abigail shook her head dismissively. "He only uses that house when he's in Brynwell for business. Now that Sir Henry has a new wife, I'm sure she would rather they lived at the Manor. It's far grander than Melbury House."

"It seems rather extravagant to keep staff at both houses," Penny commented. She couldn't imagine such wealth.

"It's not my position to question how Sir Henry chooses to manage his households." Abigail folded her hands primly on her lap and gave Penny a sharp look. "There's no point hankering after George, you know. Percival and I are hoping that Sir Henry will move us to Talbot Manor, as I'm sure his wife will want the convenience of a head coachman nearby. But George will stay in town at Melbury House if, indeed, Sir Henry still wants him at all. His new wife might make all manner of changes."

"You're not saying George might lose his job, are you?" Penny was filled with alarm. He loved working with Sir Henry's horses, and she knew he still harboured dreams of taking over Percy's position one day.

"You're worrying about nothing. Once you settle into your new life, you'll be too busy having dress fittings and social engagements to fret about a mere stable boy." She patted Penny's arm, trying to reassure her. "I'm sure Percival will make sure that George is taken care of, whatever happens. He speaks very highly of George's skill with the horses. Now, let's just enjoy today, shall we?"

Before long, they had left the crowded streets

of Brynwell behind, and the horse clopped along narrow lanes flanked by hedgerows. They were bare at the moment, but Penny could already see hints of spring with the tiny nubs of buds on the blackthorn trees.

"It's so much nicer out here in the summer," Abigail said as if reading her mind. "There's a delightful cottage next to the stable block, which would suit us very well." She sounded wistful, and Penny was in no doubt that Abigail had a promotion to live within the grounds of Talbot Manor firmly in her sights.

After about an hour, the lane started to rise gently towards the snow-covered hills that sat behind Brynwell-On-Sea. They passed through a small village and Penny's heart beat faster as she glimpsed a turret through the trees. "Are we nearly there?"

Right on cue, as Abigail nodded, Percy guided the carriage through a set of imposing wrought iron gates flanked by brick columns. The driveway wound through rolling paddocks, which were dotted with mighty oak trees, and on one side, Penny could see a herd of deer grazing. The doe-eyed creatures looked up, startled by the sound of the carriage, and bounded gracefully away. She craned her neck to look out of the other window and saw fluffy white sheep nibbling the grass through the snow and sturdy Hereford cattle lumbering along a track followed by a drover.

"This is all part of the Talbot Manor estate," Abigail said, watching Penny's delighted expression. "I expect you'll have your own horse and be able to ride across these fields one day."

Before Penny could answer, the sprawling manor house came into view, and she was speechless with awe. It was the grandest building she had ever seen, and she could scarcely believe that it was just for one family. It had a pleasing symmetry with octagonal turreted towers at either end and tall windows which glinted in the winter sun. The carriage sweep was generous enough for at least four carriages, and wide steps led up to an imposing door with a stone-carved deerhound on either side. At the centre of the sweep, there was a circular garden with an ornamental pond, and with the stable block and farm buildings, Penny thought it looked like something fit for the Queen herself.

"It's very important that you let me do the

introduction," Abigail said firmly as Percy halted the carriage outside the stables.

"I...I don't think I would even know what to say anyway." Penny loosened the scarf which George had given her, suddenly feeling overcome with nerves.

"Pin the brooch on your collar." Abigail handed it to her and watched as Penny did what she had asked.

"Is everyone ready?" Percy smiled nervously at his wife and helped them both out of the carriage. "Let's hope Sir Henry is in good spirits and everything goes to plan."

Before Penny had time to worry about what she would say, Abigail had taken her firmly by the arm and whisked her through the snow and up the steps. A stony-faced butler opened the door just as Abigail was raising her hand to knock.

"We'd like to see Sir Calder, please, Mr Plummer." Abigail's tone brooked no argument, and Penny was secretly rather impressed that she seemed so confident in the imposing surroundings.

"Is he expecting you, Mrs Webster? It ain't usual for him to take visitors without an appointment." Plummer caught sight of Penny and blinked in surprise as though he recognised her.

"We haven't made an appointment, but it's a matter of great urgency that we see him as soon as possible. I have news about Louisa..."

At the mention of her mother, Penny saw Plummer visibly pale, and a look of worry creased his brow. "Miss Louisa?" he muttered. "I hope you ain't going to upset the master, Abigail. You know it's a sore subject." He stared at Penny again, looking puzzled. "Are you related to Miss Louisa?"

"Will you just do as I've asked," Abigail hissed, pulling Penny through the door and into the grand entrance hall. "I'm sure you'll catch up on all the gossip below stairs later today, but we need to see Sir Henry, and he won't be pleased if he finds out you've kept him waiting over the news I have about his dear daughter."

Plummer shook his head at Abigail's cryptic message and hobbled away, giving Penny time to look at her surroundings. The hallway was almost as big as the whole of Willow Cottage, and a fire crackled in the huge fireplace, which was a welcome relief after the chilly carriage ride. Colourful oil paintings depicting hunting scenes lined the walls, and a gilt-framed mirror hung over the mantelpiece. A tall grandfather clock ticked loudly, and Penny heard the distant sound of footsteps hurrying as the maids went about their work.

As the minutes dragged by, Penny could tell that Abigail was growing increasingly anxious. "Perhaps he doesn't want to see us?" she whispered.

"Hush...of course he'll see us. I expect it's just Mr Plummer being slow. The man should have retired years ago, but he's like a faithful old dog who doesn't want to leave his master's side." Abigail's knuckles were white as she clutched her reticule, which almost made Penny giggle. After her kidnapping ordeal, it was pleasing to see the older woman was clearly just as nervous as Penny felt.

"Sir Henry will see you in his study," Mr Plummer told them when he eventually returned.

Penny's mouth went dry, and they followed him down the hallway before he discreetly knocked. The thought that her ma had been raised here was almost impossible for her to comprehend. She wondered whether Abigail had made a terrible mistake…one that might even end up getting them thrown off the premises and Maude losing her house. Her stomach clenched with fear as she heard a commanding voice from within the room.

"Enter."

"Mrs Webster and…the girl, to see you, Sir Henry." Plummer ushered them into the study, and Penny instantly felt more at home. The room was furnished for comfort rather than to impress, with books piled on every surface and well-worn armchairs in front of the fire. The faint aroma of cigars lingered in the air, mingling with lavender beeswax furniture polish.

"What have we here?" A grey-haired gentleman stood up slowly from behind his desk. He glanced from Abigail to Penny, and his bushy eyebrows shot up with shock. He looked as though he had seen a ghost.

"Who is this girl?" he demanded. His tone was a mixture of disbelief but also something which sounded like longing. "She looks exactly like…"

"Your daughter, Louisa?" Abigail finished for him.

Sir Henry nodded and grasped a silver-topped

walking stick to come around the desk, not taking his eyes off Penny for a moment.

"Who are you?" His voice cracked with emotion. "Is it possible that you are my daughter's child? I can scarcely believe what I'm seeing."

Louisa coughed slightly, drawing his attention back to her before Penny could reply. "I believe you are correct, Sir Henry. By very good fortune, Percival and I realised that your granddaughter has been living in Brynwell all this time. She even has a brooch to prove it." She nudged Penny with her elbow, and Penny moved her scarf to one side to reveal the brooch on her collar.

"I gave that to Louisa for her eighteenth birthday," Sir Henry gasped. "It was just a few months later that she ran away." He peered past Abigail and Penny as though expecting to see her behind them.

"I'm very sorry, but Louisa passed away six years ago," Abigail said gently.

Penny felt a surge of sympathy for her grandpapa as his face fell, and he sighed heavily. "I tried so hard never to give up hope that she might find it in her heart to come home again. Her poor mama found it much harder. The shock of Louisa running away sent her mother into a depression that she never recovered from. He looked back at Penny again and slowly brightened. "But Louisa had a daughter…and by jove, you look so much like her that it's uncanny."

"Ma banged her head the night I was born and lost her memory," Penny said shyly. "I don't think it's that she didn't want to come home to you. She just forgot who she was."

Sir Henry shook his head in astonishment and then smiled sadly. "I hope you don't think me unfeeling for not being upset about learning that Louisa passed away. The truth is, I think deep down I always knew that the fact that she didn't come home or even write to let us know she was alright meant something terrible had happened. I did my grieving long ago. But now it's like a miracle seeing you here, Penny. After all this time, this is the most wonderful gift ever—"

Abigail seized her moment and put her arm around Penny's shoulder with an ingratiating smile. "I knew you'd be happy, Sir Henry…as soon as Percival and I realised, we knew we had to return Penny to you…and what with Percival getting on a bit, we rather hoped that the reward for news about Louisa that you offered years ago might still stand…" She looked at him hopefully, and Sir Henry beamed back at her.

"You shall indeed be rewarded handsomely, Mrs Webster. Both you and your husband…just name what you want."

"Well, Percival wondered about whether you would rather we were based at Talbot Manor and we could live in the sweet cottage next to the stables," she said hastily. "And the reward money would be most helpful for when he retires. His arthritis gets terrible from sitting atop the carriage in all weathers after years of loyal service to the Calder family."

If Sir Henry was surprised by Abigail's directness in stating what she wanted, he was too happy to show it. "That's the least I can do for you and your good husband, Mrs Webster. Speak to Plummer on your way out, and he'll make sure everything is taken care of." He turned his attention back to Penny and gestured to the armchairs. "Why don't you sit down, my dear? We have a lot of catching up to do, and then I can introduce you to my new wife when she arrives later on today."

"Thank you, Sir Calder." Penny bobbed a curtsey, and the old man chuckled.

"Call me grandpapa, Penny, not Sir Calder.

You're family now." He shook his head again in disbelief. "It's like seeing Louisa come back to life. You must tell me what you've been doing all this time. I want to know every detail."

THE NEXT FEW hours passed by in a blur of talk with Sir Henry that Penny would never have believed possible. There were tears when he learned about how frail his daughter had been in her health, especially when Penny explained that Louisa had been practically destitute before Maude took her in. He hung onto every word as she described her days working for Mr Culpepper, and then he vowed to personally go and thank the Bevan family for everything they had done.

What struck Penny more than anything was how comfortable she felt in her grandpapa's presence. Far from being the uncaring, wealthy aristocrat she had heard him described as by many people in Brynwell, she discovered that he had come from humble beginnings and made his fortune shipping tea and exotic silks from India to serve the gentry of London. It was only when his first wife, Helen, had become ill from breathing in the choking smogs of London town that they moved to South Wales for her to recuperate.

"I was fortunate to buy Talbot Manor for a song," he told Penny with a twinkle in his eye. The previous owner lost a lot of money at the card tables and decided to cut his losses and move to America for a fresh start away from all his debtors. We made a gentleman's agreement at the club one night, and he sailed the following day."

"It's the most beautiful house I've ever seen," Penny said, glancing around the study.

"I made the mistake of buying it without visiting it first," Henry chuckled. "The place was in terrible disrepair when we arrived, and poor Helen almost turned right around to go straight back to London. But I purchased Melbury House in Brynwell as a temporary solution, so she had somewhere comfortable to live while this old pile was restored."

Penny sat up at the mention of Melbury House. "My best friend, George…Maude's nephew… works in the stables at Melbury House. Perhaps you've met him?"

"I must admit, even if I had, I probably wouldn't remember him." Sir Henry looked slightly shamefaced at the confession. "My head is usually filled with business matters, and the staff tend to blend into the background."

Penny gave him a rueful smile. "Someone once told me that toffs don't really notice poor folks. It sounds like they were right."

"It's something I intend to remedy now that I'm less busy with my business. I've developed an interest in the reformation of the work laws and improving the lives of the poorest in society. My wife is keen for me to get involved with politics in London, but I'm not sure whether I've left it too late."

At the mention of his new wife, Penny realised that she hadn't given any consideration to her grandpapa's new family. "What is your wife's name?" she asked.

Sir Henry's expression softened. "Juliet. You might think me an old fool, but after losing Louisa, and then my dear Helen…your grandmama… dying from a broken heart, I was in danger of becoming a lonely old man. For many years I became something of a recluse, burying myself in work because I thought there could be nobody else for me. But then I met Juliet in London, and she was like a breath of fresh air."

"I'm happy for you, Grandpapa. I wouldn't like to think of you all alone in this huge house."

"Speaking of Juliet, I'm sure she will be here any minute. She prefers the high society life of London, but I'm gradually encouraging her to enjoy country living instead. We only got married a couple of months ago, and it was something of a whirlwind romance, but she's delighted with the idea of being a titled Lady."

"Did you know her for very long?" Penny asked. She wondered curiously what her step-grandmother would be like, imagining a sweet, grey-haired lady.

"It's funny you should mention it," Sir Henry replied. "We met through my brother, who also has a house in Brynwell, but mostly lives in London." A shadow crossed his face briefly. "Edmund was the black sheep of the family. He's a solicitor, and he got embroiled in some shady deals in the past, although he's mended his ways now, thank goodness. It was Edmund who introduced Juliet to me, and now we're happily married."

"How very fortunate." Penny stifled a yawn. After her night in the warehouse, followed by the emotions of the day, she was suddenly overwhelmed with tiredness. It was cosy sitting next to the fire, and it was making her feel sleepy.

"I must introduce you to my housekeeper. She will need to get a room ready for you." Sir Henry reached for his walking stick and stood up just as there was a volley of barking from the entrance hall, which made Penny jump. "That's Bramble, my dog. He's still rather wary of Juliet, which means she must have just arrived. Come along, Penny; I need to tell her our wonderful news."

After such a pleasant few hours, Penny felt a flutter of nerves again at the thought of meeting her new step-grandmother. "Do you think she will mind me living here?" she asked hesitantly as she followed Henry out of his study.

"Mind? Of course not. She'll be delighted." He looked at Penny with a broad smile and limped ahead of her.

Mr Plummer was walking ponderously to open the large door as they arrived in the entrance hall, and Penny smiled when a black labrador jumped up from the rug in front of the fire and came bounding over to greet her.

"Hello, Bramble," she whispered, stroking the dog's velvety ears. His tongue lolled out of his mouth, making him look like he was smiling, and his tail swished back and forth against her dress as he wagged. Penny knew she'd made a new friend, although it made her miss Turk with a pang of homesickness.

"Juliet, my dear. How was the journey?" Henry smiled as an elegant woman swept into the hallway.

"Exhausting, Henry, utterly exhausting. I'm sure the springs on that coach need replacing. I expect I shall be black and blue; the lanes around here are so rough."

"I'm sorry to hear that, my sweet, and of course, I shall ask Webster to see to it at once." Henry offered Juliet his arm and drew her into the house with a wide smile.

Penny hung back in the shadows, not sure whether to introduce herself. She was shocked to see that, far from being a sweet, grey-haired old lady, her step-grandmother looked at least twenty years younger than Sir Henry and was dressed in a shot silk ruffled gown that wouldn't have looked out of place in the finest salons of London. She tugged her kid gloves off and handed them carelessly to Plummer with a peeved expression.

"I have some wonderful news to cheer you up, although I'm sure you'll hardly be able to believe it," Sir Henry continued. He beckoned Penny forwards. "This is my granddaughter, Penny Calder, my dear. After all these years of thinking I had no family of my own left other than Edmund, it turned out that dear Louisa had a little girl." He looked forlorn for a moment and then brightened again. "As I suspected, sadly, Louisa died, but Penny has come to live with us, which makes up for such a tragedy."

"You have a granddaughter?" Juliet repeated. The blood had drained from her face, and for a moment, Penny wondered if she was about to faint.

"I know...I was flabbergasted as well, but it's a miracle, Juliet. We've spent all afternoon talking, and Penny is just delightful."

"I see," Juliet said faintly. She recovered her composure and walked slowly towards Penny to shake hands. "Welcome to Talbot Manor. What a surprise this has turned out to be."

As Penny bobbed a curtsey to Juliet, she was met with a cold stare that was anything but welcoming, although Penny noticed Juliet took care to have her back to Henry so he wouldn't notice it. Penny had seen similar expressions before in the eyes of some of the women who worked at Culpepper's when they were consumed with petty jealousies over who had earned more.

"Thank you, Lady Calder," Penny said cautiously. She ventured a smile, but it wasn't returned, and Penny's heart sank. Just when she had been basking in the happy glow of Sir Henry's delight at having her at Talbot Manor, she realised that Juliet would be much harder to win over.

CHAPTER 11

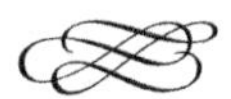

Just as Penny was getting over her worrisome introduction to her step-grandmother, there was a sudden commotion in the doorway, and Bramble let off another volley of barks which echoed around the entrance hall.

"That wretched dog is going to have to leave if he behaves like this every time we come to Talbot Manor," Juliet snapped as she turned back to Henry.

"It's only because he was so used to me being alone, dear."

Penny clicked her fingers softly by her side, and the dog stopped barking instantly, trotting back to his bed and looking up at Penny with an adoring expression.

"You see, dear. You just have to be friendly to him like Penny is doing, and he'll soon stop barking."

Two pink spots appeared on Juliet's cheeks at Henry's clumsy comment, which she felt cast her in an inferior light. "Perhaps the dog should become Penny's companion, Henry," she purred. "You know I don't really like animals, and the last thing I want is dog hairs all over my new gown. Plus, he might help Penny settle in." She pouted and fluttered her eyelashes at her new husband. "You didn't even say how lovely I look, dear. I hope Penny won't be monopolising your attention."

"You are as delightful as ever, my love," Henry replied. "I'm glad to see that you took my offer up to get some new gowns made while you were in London."

The cause for Bramble's reaction became evident as Plummer ushered two more people into the hallway.

"Come in and get warm, Annabel. And you too, Oscar," cried Henry. "Your mama tells me the carriage ride from the station was rather rough, but you're home now."

Although nobody had mentioned that Juliet had children, they looked so similar that Penny assumed that was who the additional arrivals were. She was cheered to see that Annabel was about the same age as her, and Oscar looked to be a few years older. It would be nice to have their company.

"I should have told you earlier, but we were so busy talking about the past...this is Juliet's son and daughter, Penny," Henry said. His eyes twinkled with happiness as he gestured for her to come and greet them.

Penny's cheeks flushed as everyone turned to look at her, as Henry explained who she was. "This is my long-lost granddaughter, who I've only just been reunited with today. Isn't it wonderful news? We shall all be together like one big happy family."

Plummer coughed as though he was overcome with emotion. "It will be nice to have more people under our roof again, Sir Henry," he said gruffly. "Talbot Manor will come to life again."

"I quite agree," Henry said. "And you'll be pleased to know, Penny, that Annabel is just a few months older than you, so I'm sure you'll get along."

Penny shyly regarded the girl who had golden

coiffed ringlets and was wearing a fur-trimmed cloak over her velvet travelling gown and extended her hand. "It's nice to meet you, Annabel. Your gown is very pretty."

"It is lovely, I know." Annabel's resentful expression warmed slightly at Penny's comment. "Mama insisted on buying me six new dresses because goodness knows how old-fashioned the dressmakers in Brynwell will be." She wrinkled her button nose slightly as she eyed Penny's plain green dress as if to underline her point.

"Don't be churlish, Annabel. That's not a nice way to speak about our new home." Oscar's blue eyes were amused as he stepped forward and shook Penny's hand enthusiastically. "A long-lost granddaughter? That sounds very intriguing. I'm sure we shall enjoy hearing all about your mysterious past over dinner tonight."

"It's nothing very exciting," Penny mumbled. Oscar was tall, with a sweep of dark blonde hair, and his handshake was firm. Unlike the rest of his family, he seemed genuinely pleased to meet her and Penny couldn't help but feel grateful for his kindness.

The sound of footsteps approaching saved Penny from the blush which was starting to creep over her cheeks from Oscar's interested scrutiny, and a plump woman in black bombazine and a starched white apron bustled into the hallway.

"Lawks, Mr Plummer, why didn't you tell me Lady Calder and the family had returned from London already." The woman bobbed her head apologetically. "I wasn't expecting you until later, miss, but it won't take a minute for Molly to get the fires lit in your bedroom and the parlour."

Before Juliet could reply, Sir Henry gave her a genial smile. "Mrs Pratt, I know the servants are probably already agog with our news, but you were busy when Penny arrived earlier, so I couldn't introduce you properly. This is my granddaughter. Louise...God rest her soul, had a daughter, and Penny will be living with us."

The housekeeper's mouth gaped open as Sir Henry stepped aside to reveal Penny, who had retreated to be closer to Bramble. Her jowls quivered with emotion, and she hastily crossed herself over her sturdy bosom. "It's a good thing you told me, Sir Henry; otherwise, I would have thought I'd seen a ghost. I ain't never seen the like of it...'tis as if a young miss Louisa just stepped out of the room for five minutes and then returned." She hastily dabbed a handkerchief at her eyes which had misted over with emotion.

"I really am very weary, Mrs Pratt," Juliet said with a dainty sigh. "Perhaps these sentimental reminiscences could be saved until after you've taken care of the more important things. I'd like tea and crumpets in my parlour in ten minutes and make sure Molly has aired the beds properly with the warming pans. I don't want darling Annabel to catch a cold in this draughty old place."

"Certainly, m'Lady. And I'll make up Louisa's old bedroom for Penny, so she can be next to Annabel, shall I?"

"Do whatever you wish," Juliet said with a dismissive wave of her hand. "I can feel that all these revelations are bringing on one of my headaches."

Mrs Pratt bobbed her head and hurried away with a swish of her starched skirts and one last look of astonishment at Penny over her shoulder.

As Penny followed Plummer up the grand staircase, Annabel shot her a look of cold dislike. "You needn't think that because we're the same age, we'll get along. Mama only agreed to live in this dreadful backwater to keep your grandfather happy. I already have all the friends I need in

London, where we shall return as soon as possible." She turned her nose up and marched ahead of Plummer as soon as they reached the top of the stairs, and a moment later, the upstairs landing reverberated with the sound of her bedroom door slamming.

"Take no notice of her," Plummer muttered with a long-suffering sigh. "Things ain't half changed since Sir Henry remarried, but at least we can take comfort that losing Louisa had a happier ending than we ever thought it might." He gave Penny a small wink. "Perhaps you'll help that little madam have some better manners," he added.

A FEW WEEKS LATER, Penny hurried along the corridor upstairs and arrived breathlessly in what had been the old nursery, with Bramble at her heels. The clock was just chiming nine as she burst through the door, and her cheeks were pink from a brisk walk she had just taken in the garden, enjoying the swathe of crocuses which were flowering where the snow had finally melted.

"Please can Bramble sit with us, Miss Evans?

He'll be as quiet as a mouse, you won't even know he's here."

The new governess, who Sir Henry had taken on, eyed the dog as she tidied a stack of books on her desk. "It's not my usual arrangement, but I suppose I can allow it as long as he doesn't distract you and Annabel from your studies."

Penny patted Bramble's head and then settled at her desk, eager to start learning. When Sir Henry had asked about her education shortly after her arrival, he had been shocked to discover that work at Culpepper's brickyard had taken priority over attending the poor school. So much so that he had hastily added child labour practices to his list of things to discuss with influential parliamentarians the next time he was in London.

A few days later, Miss Evans had been summoned for an interview and was now living in the servant's quarters with the rest of the staff, much to her delight. Her last ten years had been spent trying to instil some sort of education in the large brood of children belonging to a merchant who lived in Ceylon. Although she had been sad when the position came to an end, she was glad to leave the stifling heat behind and return home to Wales, and the thought of working for the wealthy

Calder family was appealing, with just two young ladies to teach.

"Where is Annabel?" Miss Evens asked.

"I think Molly just went to her room to get her up." Penny looked slightly embarrassed on Annabel's behalf. Usually, by this time of day, Penny would have done several hours of work at the brickyard, but Annabel was not an early riser.

"We will start with some history and then go on to study literature when she arrives."

Miss Evans was starting to get the measure of her two charges. Despite her lack of formal education, Penny was a quick learner, and she had confided that her ma had done what she could to teach her herself with Maude's books. The governess could tell that Penny wanted to make up for lost opportunities and displayed a bright mind and an innate curiosity about the subjects they had covered already.

Annabel could not have been more different, and she reminded Miss Evans of the oldest of her previous pupils who had resented every hour spent in the classroom.

"We start at nine o'clock sharp, Annabel." Miss Evans tried to strike a balance of firmness but kindness as the girl sidled in a few minutes before ten. She knew that it was probably as hard for Annabel as it was for Penny to adapt to a new life far away from London, which was why she was trying to be understanding. "Penny has already done almost an hour on her history lesson, but we saved literature because I know it's your favourite subject."

Annabel stifled a yawn and reluctantly opened her book of poetry. "I only like it because it's not about stuffy battles. Can we read some romantic poems, please, Miss Evans?"

"There are more topics than just romance to consider, Annabel. What about nature?"

Annabel pouted and tossed her golden ringlets. "Why would I want to know about animals and trees? Mama says that all this time spent poring over books might give me frown lines and make me short-sighted."

"But there's so much to discover," Penny said. She couldn't believe that Annabel wasn't interested. "Take the manor's estate, for instance. If we learn about nature, we will understand the farm better and the garden. Those are all important for the future of Talbot Manor."

Annabel shuddered in horror at the mention of the farm. "That's what we have the estate workers for, Penny. I'm not some sort of peasant, so why do I need to learn about cattle and sheep?"

"Grandpapa says it's very interesting," Penny shot back. "And I asked him if Miss Evans can teach us about how tea is grown in India and how silk is made, so we can understand more about his business."

"Really, Penny, you're filling your head with nonsense. The only animals I'm interested in are horses. I've already asked Mr Webster if he can find me a nice dappled grey mare, so I look pretty when I'm out riding. And I might learn how to arrange flowers if it will help me marry well, but all of these boring facts that Miss Evans is intent on teaching us are a waste of time."

Miss Evans clapped her hands sharply to break up the quarrel that was brewing. "There are plenty of poems that combine romance and nature. Let's start with those, and then we can move on to arithmetic after luncheon."

"It's all so dull," Annabel muttered, resting her chin on her hand and gazing out of the window.

"The mistress of a large house needs to be able to manage the household budget," Miss Evans said crisply. "It's something a future husband would want to know you could do…as well as being able to talk to guests in an entertaining manner."

Framing the lessons in how they might help Annabel marry well caught her attention, and soon peace was restored as the lesson progressed.

By the time the clock chimed twelve, Annabel was becoming restless again. "Haven't we done enough now, Miss Evans? I would rather be practising the piano." Her face took on a dreamy expression as she thought about the handsome piano teacher, Mr Phipps, who had started coming once a week.

Miss Evans shook her head and tried another tack. "You know Sir Henry said no piano practice until after all your lessons are complete." Looking at the stubborn set of Annabel's mouth, she was starting to revise her thoughts about her new position being a comfortable way to eke out her last few years until retirement.

"The quicker we do our studies, the quicker you can get onto other things," Penny said. Annabel's attitude was irritating her. "Don't you realise how lucky we are to have Miss Evans? The children at Culpepper's would have given anything to be sitting in a nice warm classroom, with a kind teacher helping them better themselves, and all you do is complain."

Annabel's expression was mutinous. "I wish you'd never come here, Penny Frost."

A sudden tap at the door interrupted the argument, and Molly poked her head into the room. "Mrs Pratt would like to see you, Miss Evans. Summat' about menu preparation lessons for the young ladies."

The governess nodded. "I'd like you to write two paragraphs about the poem we have just studied, please, girls, describing how the author wanted the reader to feel."

As soon as Miss Evans had left the room, Annabel threw down her book and pushed her chair back. "I don't even know why I'm being forced to spend my time with you, Penny," she said. A resentful scowl marred her pretty features. "Mama thinks it's a disgrace, making me share lessons with someone who was lugging filthy bricks for a living just a few weeks ago."

"At least I know the value of getting an education," Penny retorted. She knew that Annabel looked down on her, but to hear it stated so boldly was hurtful.

"Mama says you were living in one of those

scruffy little houses on Sketty Lane. Why can't you just go back there? Ever since you arrived, Sir Henry is always talking about how wonderful Louisa was and how lucky it was to find you instead of being grateful that Mama and I are here."

Penny's cheeks flushed at Annabel's careless words. "The house at Sketty Lane might have been scruffy, but at least Maude and the Bevans were kindhearted instead of being full of airs and graces like you."

Annabel jumped up so suddenly that her chair toppled over, making Bramble leap off his bed. "You're just a selfish, common girl, Penny," she shouted. "Mama promised that I would be the apple of Sir Henry's eye, but you've spoiled everything."

"That's not fair. I've spent all my life wondering who my real family are. I can't help it if Grandpapa is pleased that we've been reunited."

"You're always showing me up…trying to make me look bad in front of Miss Evans." Annabel was working herself up into a temper, and her voice rose to a screech. "You're just a nobody…why don't you leave us all alone and go back to the gutter where you belong."

Bramble leapt to Penny's side, and he started to growl protectively. "It's alright," Penny said soothingly.

"Everyone likes you better than me…even that wretched dog." Annabel rushed past Penny to leave, but suddenly there was a terrible tearing sound as her silk gown caught on the upturned chair.

"Girls! What is the meaning of this?" Miss Evans hurried into the room with a shocked expression, taking in Bramble's raised hackles and the ragged rip in Annabel's expensive dress. "I only left you for a few minutes, and I expect you to behave in a civilised manner, not use it as an excuse to argue."

"What is going on, Miss Evans?" Juliet appeared in the doorway, clutching her head with a pained look on her face. "I was trying to take a nap as I have a dreadful headache, but then it sounded like there were a couple of fishwives having a row." Her eyes narrowed with anger as she saw Annabel's dress.

"It's all her fault, Mama." Tears pooled in Annabel's blue eyes, and she hurried to stand next to her mother. "Penny called me some dreadful names and then set Bramble on me."

"I…I did no such thing—"

"Wait until your grandpapa hears about this," Juliet snapped, holding her hand up to stop Penny from saying anything else. "If I had my way, you wouldn't even be here, but I won't have you ruining everything for my darling Annabel. Go to your room and take that mangy animal with you."

"Shouldn't we at least hear Penny's side of the story, Lady Calder?" Miss Evans said hesitantly.

"Are you saying that my dear daughter is lying?" Juliet gave the governess a cold stare. "Annabel has been raised with manners and decorum, unlike Penny, who is of a questionable background. I'll thank you to remember your place in future."

Miss Evans nodded and busied herself at her desk, not wanting to risk her position. "Perhaps we shall resume our lessons tomorrow morning, girls," she said quietly.

Annabel shot Penny a triumphant look over her shoulder as Juliet linked arms with her. "Come along, my dear," Juliet said. "Why don't you try my jewellery on until it's time for luncheon, and then we could look through some of my old magazines. I shall have to ask Henry to make sure we receive

The Young Ladies Journal from London, so we don't get too out of touch."

As Penny walked back to her room, her heart felt heavy. She longed for the simple company of Nell and Jacob, teasing each other in the homely front parlour at Willow Cottage, and Maude chatting about the latest news from their friends and neighbours. But more importantly, she missed George. Losing his uncomplicated friendship, which had been blossoming into something more, was like a dull ache in her heart that never went away. She was learning that exchanging a life of poverty for one of ease and wealth had not come without its costs.

"Come along, Bramble. You'll keep me company, won't you?"

The dog nuzzled at Penny's hand when she sat in the window seat in her bedroom to stare forlornly out of the window. She could see Percy Webster leading some horses out to the paddock with one of the stable boys, and she wished that it could have been George. If Annabel was determined for them never to be friends, it was going to make her time at Talbot Manor harder than she could have imagined.

* * *

"GOODNIGHT, GRANDPAPA." Penny excused herself from the drawing room later that night after spending a quiet hour reading near the fire. Juliet had been frosty with her during dinner, and Annabel had eaten in her room, claiming that she didn't feel well. Penny was just relieved that her grandfather hadn't seemed to notice the strained atmosphere as he had been too busy jovially telling Juliet about some of his travels to exotic parts of India when he first started the business.

"Goodnight, Penny." Henry gave her an amused look as Bramble stood up to follow her. "I can see he considers himself to be your dog now," he chuckled. "So much for being loyal to his master."

"He's very lovely," Penny said, ruffling the dog's ears.

Juliet frowned as she reached for her cup of tea, and Penny thought for one terrible moment she was going to accuse Bramble of ripping Annabel's dress in front of Sir Henry. "If the maids complain about dog hairs in your bedroom, you'll have to help them clean up."

Penny nodded, thinking it was a small price to pay. "Yes, Juliet, of course," she said.

Her lamp cast tall shadows as she trudged upstairs after going to the kitchen to say good-night to Mrs Pratt. It had taken Penny a while to get used to the layout of the manor, with all its narrow passages and multitude of rooms, and there were still parts she had yet to explore, but it was at least starting to feel a bit more like home.

As she passed Annabel's bedroom, she heard a noise from within that made her stop. Bramble lifted one ear and cocked his head to the side, hearing it too. It was the sound of muffled sobs.

"Annabel? Are you alright?" Penny knocked gently on the door, but there was no answer, and the sobs grew even louder. She turned the handle and peeked around to look into the room.

"What's wrong, Annabel? I'm sorry about earlier. I never wanted us to fall out with each other." Penny hurried over to the bed where Annabel was face down on the silk coverlet. "I know you're missing all your friends, but I promise I didn't mean to upset you."

Annabel rolled over and sat up, dabbing a lace handkerchief on her tear-stained cheeks. "That's just it…I…I don't have any friends…" A fresh wave of sobs engulfed her, and Bramble jumped up onto the bed and lay his head on her lap, looking up at her with mournful brown eyes.

"But I thought you said you'd left them all behind in London, and you couldn't wait to go back?" Penny gave her a hesitant smile, not wanting to make the situation any worse.

"I was only ten when my papa died, and because he didn't leave us very well provided for, Mama had to take a position as a companion for a wealthy lady who was rather frail. The people who I thought were my friends all turned their backs on us." Annabel's voice wavered again.

"I'm sorry to hear that. What a mean thing to do just because your circumstances changed."

"When Mama told us she was marrying Sir Henry, I thought people might want to be friends with me again, but then we came to live here, and I've been so…lonely."

Penny realised with a jolt of surprise that the two of them were not so different. "I miss my old family too," she said quietly. "It was hard work at the brickyard, but Maude and her family always treated me as one of their own."

"I didn't mean what I said about your work or that you belong in the gutter," Annabel said, having the grace to look rather shamefaced. "I'm not spoilt…well, maybe just a little. I'd like to hear more about it. I don't know how you managed to get up to start work at six o'clock."

"We didn't have much choice. Let me tell you all about Mr Culpepper…he was the most miserly man you could ever wish to meet. One day, he was in a high temper about losing his handkerchief, and it was in the middle of winter, and his nose would never stop dripping…" Penny found she was able to talk about her past without the wrench of sadness she had felt before, and soon Annabel was smiling again, which gave Penny a glimmer of hope that perhaps it was the beginning of a friendship forged out of necessity for both of them.

As the clock ticked on the mantelshelf and the fire in the hearth cast a cosy glow over the room, Bramble looked between the two girls and then lowered his head with a contented sigh before falling fast asleep.

CHAPTER 12

Penny smiled happily to herself as she unlatched the gate of the walled garden and let herself in. Gathering flowers to arrange throughout the manor house was one of her favourite pastimes to while away the time, and she never failed to appreciate just how fortunate she was to be afforded such a luxury. It was late summer, and the air was filled with the heady fragrance of damask roses and the soporific buzz of bees. Butterflies drifted between the blooms, and she smiled as she paused for a moment to watch a gaggle of birds splashing in one of the shallow rills of water that ran through the garden. Bramble lolloped along behind her, sniffing enthusiastically before flopping under the shade of the apple trees for another snooze.

As she methodically snipped flowers and foliage to lay in her trug, Penny's thoughts turned to the days ahead. It would be Annabel's nineteenth birthday at the end of the week, and all she could talk about was the upcoming ball at Sir Peregrine Walker's grand country house.

"Anyone would think it was the only thing that mattered," she commented to Bramble, who opened one eye and lazily wagged his tail.

The calm oasis of the walled garden gave Penny a chance to escape for a while from Juliet's mercurial moods. Ever since Penny had arrived at Talbot Manor almost five years ago, she had always sensed an undercurrent of resentment from her grandfather's second wife, as though she thought of Penny as a cuckoo in the nest, usurping Juliet's position in the house. Penny tried to remain slightly in the background, always making sure that Annabel took centre stage during social gatherings. Over the years, Penny and Annabel had become firm friends, although Annabel could still be careless at times, reminding Penny of her lower-class upbringing. And Penny had endeavoured to do her best to please Juliet, to keep a fragile peace within the house. The truth was, she was pleased that her grandfather had found love again, but lately, as Sir Henry had grown older and the age gap between him and Juliet seemed more pronounced, she had occasionally sensed that Juliet seemed rather lacklustre in her affection towards him. Penny had even wondered whether the marriage had been one of convenience. An escape for Juliet and a way to secure her place in high society with a wealthy husband. She hoped not because the thought of her grandpapa being used in such a way left a bad taste in her mouth.

"Do you need any help, miss?" One of the gardeners stopped on his way to the orangery and put his barrow down. "You can cut as many flowers as you like; they won't last much longer, what with autumn being just around the corner."

"Thank you, Bob." Penny gave him a cheery wave and then glanced guiltily up at the windows of the manor house, hoping that Juliet wasn't watching. After being raised by Maude, Penny often felt as though she straddled two different worlds. She felt just at home chatting with the gardeners and the maids as when she was at a tea party with some of Sir Henry's important guests. He told her it was something to be grateful for, but

Juliet disliked it, saying that Penny was causing confusion by being so friendly to the staff.

"It makes the maids think they can be over-familiar with us," she had complained to Sir Henry one day after catching Penny talking to Molly about how her little sister was feeling with a bout of the flu.

"I don't agree, my dear," Henry had countered, not noticing his wife's look of annoyance. "Penny has that rare quality which allows her to empathise with those who are less well-off than us because she understands what it's like to have to work for every farthing and to go hungry when times are hard. I find her insights very informative for my philanthropic works."

Juliet had sniffed disparagingly. "You've worked hard to elevate your social status, Henry dear. We should be enjoying your wealth, not feeling guilty about every pauper who is too idle to make something of themselves."

Penny had wanted to explain that most of the people she had grown up with had been the very opposite of lazy, but she knew it would fall on deaf ears where Juliet was concerned. She was clearly intent on distancing herself from the working classes she had so nearly become sucked into when her first husband had died, and always tried to change the conversation whenever Henry wanted to talk about reform.

Once her trug was full, Penny returned to the house, strolling into the servants' quarters to fill up some buckets with clean, cold water to give the flowers a good drink and refresh them before starting her arranging.

"I hope you didn't put your face in the sun, miss?" Daphne Fraser, the cook, had a mop of fiery red hair and lived in fear of getting freckles.

"I did take my bonnet off for a while," Penny confessed with a wry smile. "It was just so nice to feel the breeze after the hot summer we've had, but I'm sure the odd freckle won't matter to me."

"Ain't you going to the ball with Miss Annabel?" Daphne asked curiously.

"You know I don't like these grand social affairs," Penny replied. She made a new slanted snip on the stem of each bloom before placing them carefully into her buckets. "I prefer grandpapa's small gatherings where I can listen to the conversations about social reform instead of the interminable gossip about marriage proposals that everyone seems to talk about at balls."

Daphne chuckled. "You and Miss Annabel are

like chalk and cheese, 'tis remarkable that you get along so well, although I remember it wasn't always the case. That pretty little nose of hers was put right out of joint when you first arrived."

"I'm sure that's why we are such good friends now." Penny grinned as she remembered the incident in the schoolroom when poor Miss Evans had been convinced that Bramble had ripped Annabel's dress. Thankfully, it had all been smoothed over within a few days, although Annabel had never really applied herself to her studies, much to Miss Evans' disappointment. "If we were too alike, Annabel would probably find me rather irritating. I suppose we each have our own interests and strengths," she added diplomatically.

"You're very much like your ma, God rest her soul." Daphne frowned with concentration as she piped the last few swirls of icing onto Annabel's birthday cake and then tied a ribbon around it to finish it off.

"I like to hear about her." Penny sighed wistfully, wishing she could have known what her mother had been like in Talbot Manor. Had she been kind to the staff? Did she enjoy flower arranging as well? So much of Penny's past was still a mystery, but she had gradually accepted that there was nothing she could do to change it.

"She used to like coming into the kitchen as well," Daphne said conversationally. "I think she was lonely sometimes, rattling around in this big house. Your grandpapa was busy with the business, and your grandmama's health was often poor. She would retire to her bed for days at a time, which left Louisa at a loose end after she'd finished her lessons."

"What did she do to fill her time?" Penny hoped that Daphne was in a talkative mood.

"You have to remember that I was just a young scullery maid then, but your ma was always very kind to all of us. She had a lovely pony and used to ride across the parkland, and she was forever in the garden. That's when all the trouble started—" Daphne flushed and stopped talking abruptly as Penny gave her a sharp look.

"Trouble? What do you mean?"

"Didn't your grandpapa ever explain why Louisa ran away?" Daphne continued slowly.

"He said it was due to a romance, but then Juliet interrupted and said there was no point in dragging up the past."

"Well, I reckon you're old enough to know the

truth now, miss." Daphne wrestled with her conscience for a moment. "If I tell you, though, I could get into trouble."

"It won't go any further than the two of us," Penny reassured her. "I think grandpapa would happily tell me, but I don't like to ask in case it upsets him."

"It's nothing sordid like Lady Juliet likes to imply." Daphne looked offended at the thought of Juliet saying unkind things about Louisa. "Your ma fell in love with one of the gardeners. Jack Hastings. He was a good-looking fellow and kindhearted too. He was forever looking after rescued animals…birds with broken wings, that sort of thing. The old cook tried to warn your ma not to go down that route because of their difference in social class. Your grandpapa would never have agreed to them being together if he'd found out."

"Did Jack treat Ma nicely?" A sudden vision of George floated into her mind. It was a while since she had seen him, but she still remembered the tender kiss he had given her when they went ice skating and the way it had made her feel.

"Oh, yes. He was head over heels in love with her." Daphne smiled at the memory. "He used to bring her little nosegays of flowers and always saved the best fruit from the garden for her."

"So what happened? Why did she leave without telling anyone where she was going?"

"Sir Henry found out that they were in love and forbade Louisa from seeing him again. Jack was told he had to leave Talbot Manor and find work elsewhere. Poor Louisa…she cried for hours that day."

Penny's heart went out to her mother, although she knew that Henry would not have done it out of malice. It simply wasn't acceptable for his daughter to marry below her class, and it would have made her a social outcast.

"The trouble was that Sir Henry underestimated how determined Louisa was to be with Jack. They ran away together that night. She might have already been in the family way…it was in the summer, and I recall there was a terrible thunderstorm. By the time Sir Henry and Lady Helen realised the following morning that she was gone, it was too late."

"But when Mama had me, she was all alone." Penny felt a crushing disappointment that her father had turned out not to be the kind man she had hoped him to be.

Daphne gave Penny a reassuring pat on her shoulder. "None of us knew where they went, and I don't think Sir Henry ever forgave himself if it's any consolation. But don't think badly of your pa, Penny. We assumed he must have abandoned Louisa, but it wasn't so. One snowy night in December, it would have been not long before you were born, the coalman told us that Jack had been killed in an accident at the docks. He'd been working hard to try and do right by your ma, but tragically it wasn't do be."

"And Ma never came home because she feared grandpapa turning her away again, especially if he knew she was with child." Penny's eyes misted over with unshed tears, which she dashed away before giving Daphne a grateful smile.

"I hope I ain't upset you?" The cook looked worried that she had said too much.

"No, Daphne. Not in the least. I've always feared that Mama was badly treated or that my pa was some sort of scoundrel. Finding out about Jack has set my mind at rest."

"You're not disappointed that he was just a lowly gardener?"

Penny shook her head, thinking about George

again. "We can't help who we fall in love with, I suppose."

"You have a wise head on those young shoulders of yours," Daphne replied with a chuckle. "Speaking of love, Annabel came looking for you a little while ago. She wants you to help her plan her outfit for the ball this afternoon."

"I'm not sure that I'm the best person for that task, but I'll do my best." Penny put her flowers in the cool of the scullery until she would have time to arrange them later. She still had an hour until lunch would be served, so she decided to spend the time with her grandfather. He had been complaining of feeling tired recently, so she plucked a single dusky maroon rose from her collection and put it in a bud vase to cheer him up.

"I HOPE you're not working too hard, Grandpapa. You know the doctor said you should be taking things a little easier since your rheumatic fever last winter." Penny placed the rose on Henry's desk. "Shall I pour the coffee that Molly brought for you before it goes cold?"

Sir Henry gave his granddaughter an absent-minded nod. "Thank you, Penny, that would be lovely. I've been busy preparing for my first speech in Parliament. Would you like to hear what it's about?"

Penny nodded eagerly. "It was kind of Sir Peregrine to help secure you a place, although I'm worried that it might be too much for you, what with having to travel up to London more often."

"It's the only way to effect change, Penny. I can talk about reform until I'm blue in the face, but I have to be in London to persuade the people who will change the laws. Sir Peregrine has been a Member of Parliament for a while, so I'm sure he will guide me through what needs to be done."

Penny felt a surge of affection for her grandfather as he read out the points he wanted to talk about. She enjoyed listening to him talking about his work, and he had always encouraged her to provide her own thoughts on the subject, unlike most men of his class who expected ladies to only discuss fashion and household matters.

"What do you think?" he asked her as he presented his conclusion. "We are pushing for more sanitary conditions in factories and to raise the age of children working in such places."

"It's a good start, Grandpapa," Penny said thoughtfully. "You have to make sure that working people are paid a fair wage if this is to succeed, though. Maude had to take us to work at Culpepper's brickworks, as did all the parents because otherwise, she wouldn't have earnt enough to put food on the table and pay the rent."

Sir Henry took a sip of his coffee and nodded. "I'm ashamed that I didn't even know what was happening in my own brickworks, although, in my defence, I expected Mr Culpepper, as the manager, to treat his workers decently."

"At least more of the children are now receiving some schooling since you raised the wages." Penny smiled. Persuading her grandfather to do that had been one of the proudest moments of her life, which Maude had thanked her profusely for.

"I need to sign all these business letters now." Henry sighed wearily as he pulled a stack of vellum papers towards him and uncapped his fountain pen to dip the nib in ink.

"I'll blot them for you if that will help you get the job done faster." Penny drew up a chair, and they worked together. Henry had a distinctive signature that ended in a flourish which reminded Penny of the swirl on the family coat of arms. She wondered if that was done deliberately or just the way he had always signed his name.

After a concerted effort, the task was done, and Henry leaned back in his chair. "You're a good girl, Penny. You take after your mama in so many ways."

Penny turned pink at the unexpected praise. "Grandpapa...I hope you won't be cross...but I know about who my father was." She waited for Henry's expression to change, but he just gave her a nod.

"I guessed one of the servants would tell you in time. I should have done it myself, but I was too cowardly, Penny. I'm sorry. I will always regret telling Louisa that she couldn't see Jack anymore. I should have seen how in love she was and trusted her to make the choices which were right for her."

"You were concerned for her, Grandpapa, that's all." She rested her hand lightly over Henry's. "I was just glad that he tried his best to look after Mama. You mustn't blame yourself for what happened. Mama could be stubborn...or determined, as Maude liked to say."

"You're right about that." Henry chuckled. "She was always headstrong, and I see that in you as well, in the way you're determined to help me be a better employer." He grasped his walking stick and stood up stiffly. "There's something I've been meaning to show you."

Penny's interest was piqued, and she offered him her elbow. He was unsteady on his feet after sitting for so long, and she didn't want him to lose his balance.

"Louisa was always terribly impatient, but she loved to embroider. She used to stitch beautiful miniature samplers, and after she left, I had our master carpenter make a special box for me, and he inlaid one of the samplers into the lid. It's just in here, see."

Penny watched with amazement as Henry bent down and reached under one of the shelves of his bookcase, fumbling for something. There was a soft click, and suddenly a section of the shelf sprang open to reveal a secret compartment.

"Don't tell anyone," Henry said with a small wink. "It's only sentimental things that I keep in there. Take it out and have a look, and it can be our little secret."

Penny knelt down and pulled the carved wooden box out, tracing her fingers over the fine stitching of her mother's embroidery, which depicted the coat of arms surrounded by tiny sprigs of violets and primroses. It was exquisite and explained why Louisa had always been so good at doing dressmaking repairs, even when she became frail and unwell. Inside there was an old silver locket, which had belonged to Lady Helen, and a scruffy stuffed toy which had been Louisa's when she was a little girl, as well as a few other trinkets. Underneath everything was a thick document, sealed with red wax and tied in a thin red ribbon. It looked like some sort of official document, but before Penny could ask her grandfather what it was, the sound of hoofbeats and the rumble of carriage wheels outside announced someone's arrival, and Bramble scampered to the door, scratching to leave.

"That must be Oscar, home on leave." She hastily packed the box up again and put it back in the hidden compartment before closing the front. As if by magic, it looked just like a normal part of the bookcase again, and if she hadn't seen Henry open it with her own eyes, she never would have believed it was there.

"How lovely, he'll be able to come to the ball with us. Annabel and Juliet will be pleased." Henry hobbled after Penny, who was already hurrying to welcome Oscar back from his latest trip to India in The Royal Artillery.

Just as Penny got to the entrance hall, Annabel ran lightly down the stairs. In spite of routinely declaring that Oscar was exceedingly annoying as an older brother, she missed him when he was away on duty, as did Penny. He had grown into a kind, thoughtful young man, and his good looks set many hearts a-flutter when he was home.

"Why is Webster taking so long to park the carriage?" Annabel checked her appearance in the mirror while they waited. "Do you think I'm getting freckles on my nose?" she demanded, pulling Penny over to join her. "The one time I want to look my best at the ball, and this wretched sunshine has made me look like a peasant who toils out in the fields all day. How am I ever going to find a husband looking like this?"

"Welcome home, Captain Calder." Plummer's voice rose in alarm. "Blimey, sir…whatever happened to you out there?"

"What is it?" Penny turned around, shocked to hear a slow shuffle instead of the usual sound of his confident footsteps striding into the hallway."

"Oscar…you're wounded." Annabel's shriek

brought all the maids running as she and Penny ran to help him up the steps.

"We were doing so well, but then I got hit by a dratted stray shot…got me in the leg, and then the wound became infected." Oscar's face was grey with fatigue as he leaned on his crutches. "Not to worry…the doctor said I was lucky not to lose my leg…but it means I probably won't be on active duty again."

"Don't just stand there, Annabel. Get your brother a chair." Mrs Pratt clucked over Oscar like a worried mother hen, issuing instructions to the maids to make up the old study into a temporary bedroom while Annabel and Plummer dragged an armchair across for him to sit in.

"They should be ashamed of themselves, harming one of the Calders," Mrs Pratt said indignantly. "Lawks…if I got my hands on them, they'd soon know about it. Never mind, Master Oscar, you're back home now, and we'll soon get you better again."

"I'm sorry it had to end this way," Penny said gently, tucking a rug over his knee a few minutes later.

Oscar shrugged, but there was regret in his blue eyes. "All I ever wanted was to be in the Artillery.

I'm not sure what I'll do now if I'm discharged." He gave Penny a rueful smile. "At least I'll have news of the ball to take my mind off it for a few weeks. Annabel already told me a moment ago that she intends to find a husband there."

Their eyes met, and they both chuckled. "It's good to have you home, Oscar," Penny said. "We've missed you, and perhaps you underestimate what else you're capable of. But for now, you must rest and get completely better; otherwise, we'll never hear the end of it from Mrs Pratt."

CHAPTER 13

Annabel peered out of the window at the low scudding clouds and then pulled a face as a sudden squall of rain rattled against the glass.

"Why couldn't it have stayed dry for the ball?" she grumbled. "This sort of weather makes my hair misbehave. If ever there was a night I want to look my best, it's tonight."

"Maybe the rain will have blown over by this evening." Penny was admiring the shot silk of Annabel's dress. Even in the grey autumnal light, it shimmered like peacock feathers. "Besides, Sir Peregrine's son won't care if you have a few extra curls," she added mischievously.

Annabel turned back from the window with a

dreamy expression. "It was an unexpected treat to learn that Benedict Walker was returning to Brynwell for the ball. When he rode over to ask after Sir Henry's health, he told me that he had grown weary of London and might even stay here permanently."

"He's nothing like his father if that's the case. Grandpapa says that Sir Peregrine thrives on the cut and thrust of Parliament and finds managing his estate here rather tedious." Penny thought privately that Benedict would make a good match for Annabel. He was handsome in a rakish way, but rumour had it that he had already broken several hearts in London while he had been managing his father's business interests up there for the last few years. She hoped Annabel wouldn't end up getting the same treatment.

"He asked if we could have the first dance at the ball when he was leaving." Annabel twirled happily, but then a look of doubt came over her face. "I'm worried that I won't know many people there, Penny. Apparently, a lot of the guests are from London. What if I get nervous and make a fool of myself?"

"That won't happen," Penny replied, giving her friend a reassuring smile. "You can hold your own against any of the high society ladies, I'm sure." She was surprised that Annabel was feeling anxious. Usually, she brimmed with confidence, and Penny wondered if it was a lingering sense of inadequacy from the way her friends had turned their backs on her all those years ago because of sheer snobbery.

Annabel looked unconvinced, and her beautiful features were marred by a worried frown. "I really do like Benedict, Penny. I know you're worried that he might dally with my affections, but this could be my only chance to make a good impression on him."

"If he's staying here, you have time to take things slowly, don't you?"

"But what if he sees someone better than me this evening?" Annabel's voice was starting to rise, and Penny knew that tears might not be far away. "It's impossible to meet the sort of gentleman Mama wants me to marry stuck out in the countryside as we are. The only chance I have is at church. But Benedict would be perfect. With their estate and his father's connections..." Her words drifted off, and she didn't need to state that her future would be secure.

"You don't need to get so het up about it,

Annabel. Grandpapa will always make sure that Juliet is well taken care of, which means that you and Oscar will be as well. He loves your ma very much." Penny tried to ignore the thought that Juliet might not love Sir Henry in an equal measure. She had barely seen them together in the last few weeks because he hadn't been feeling well, and Juliet seemed distracted, complaining about the smallest thing.

"You're right." Annabel sat at her dressing table and started trying different ribbons in her hair to see which she liked best. "Mama always said to us that she would inherit Talbot Manor right from when she agreed to Sir Henry's marriage proposal. I know I don't have to worry about being financially secure, Penny; it's just that I want to marry for love, not like—" She stopped abruptly. "Never mind...what I'm really saying is, will you please change your mind and come to the ball with me tonight?"

"I don't have anything to wear, and we both know that your ma wants you to be the centre of attention. I think she was quite relieved when I said I would stay at home to look after Grandpapa."

"Don't worry about Mama. I'll tell her I need

you to come for moral support." Annabel jumped up and hurried to her wardrobe. "You can borrow one of my old gowns. We're about the same size."

Penny knew that she wouldn't get a moment's peace unless she agreed to Annabel's request. Even though she had initially said she didn't want to go, the air of excitement over the last few days had become infectious, and she had found herself wishing she could be included. "Has Oscar agreed to chaperone you?" she asked. He had made a remarkable recovery in the few weeks he had been home, thanks to Mrs Pratt's devoted attention and an array of nourishing meals cooked by Daphne, who was determined to see him restored to his former self.

"Yes, although he was worried that people might bombard him with questions about why he's walking with a stick. He'll have to sit out the dances, of course." She shot Penny a smile. "You see...if you come with us, he'll have someone to talk to while I'm dancing with Benedict."

"Alright, you've persuaded me." Penny laughed as Annabel started pulling gowns out of her wardrobe. "They're all the wrong colour for me. You know that you suit pale colours with your blonde hair, but they make me look as if I haven't slept for a week."

"Well, you can't go in one of your day gowns; they're far too plain." Annabel wrinkled her nose as she eyed the practical linsey-woolsey dress that Penny was wearing.

"I shall wear one of my ma's dresses," Penny said firmly. If she was going to accompany Annabel, she wanted to at least decide what she would wear. "Mrs Pratt kept them in perfect condition in case Ma ever came home again. They just need a little airing and perhaps some minor alterations, which Molly is more than capable of doing. She had the same hair colour as me, so they will be more suitable."

"But won't they look rather old-fashioned?" Annabel held up one of her pale yellow gowns against Penny and cocked her head to one side. "You're right," she muttered. "This does nothing to enhance your looks."

"They're not as fashionable as yours, but that's all the more reason for all eyes to be on you tonight, Annabel, which is what we want, isn't it? Just think of Benedict sweeping you around the dance floor and all the other young men wondering who the beauty is he's dancing with. I shall happily blend into the background and keep Oscar company."

"You're the best sort of friend I could have wished for." Annabel threw her arms around Penny's shoulders and gave her a hug. "Promise we'll always look out for each other, Penny?"

"You don't ever need to ask that. Your so-called friends might have deserted you in the past, but I'm not that sort of person. Now, I need to ask Molly to fetch her sewing basket, and you must rest if you're to make a good impression tonight." Penny hurried away with a spring in her step. She knew exactly which gown would suit her, and despite her initial reluctance, she was looking forward to the night ahead, with good company and perhaps a few dances if she was lucky.

After an enjoyable hour with Molly, who was surprisingly skilful with a needle and thread, Penny stood in front of the tall, gilt-edged mirror in her bedroom and gave a satisfied nod. The gown of Louisa's she had chosen was a ruby-red velvet, which showed off her curves, but the neckline sat modestly so as not to reveal too much of her décolletage. Molly had taken in the waist with a couple of tucks, and now the length and fit were perfect.

"I'd like to add some lace trim to the sleeves, and Mrs Pratt told me she still has some seed pearls that were Lady Helen's, which would look lovely sewn on the bodice." Molly's eyes were sparkling with the unexpected treat of being able to indulge her dress-making skills instead of helping to cook lunch.

"Your talents are wasted being a maid," Penny said, turning this way and that, holding her hair up.

Molly blushed. "My Ma taught me what she knew, but it was easier to get a job as a maid because she knew Mrs Pratt would look after me, and we needed the money."

"I'll ask Sir Henry if you might be spared for an hour a day to hone your skills. I'm sure there are plenty of opportunities for you to mend things in the manor, and perhaps Mrs Pratt will give some of your chores to the scullery maid instead. That way, it's a chance for everyone to progress."

"I wish you were the mistress of the house instead of Lady Juliet," Molly blurted out. She hastily covered her mouth with her hand. "Don't tell her I said that, Miss Penny. It's just that Lady

Juliet is always saying I'm clumsy, whereas you treat us all ever so much nicer."

"I'm afraid you'll have to get used to Lady Juliet's ways. She will be the mistress of the house even after Grandpapa is no longer with us."

"Yes, miss. If I can have the gown now, I should finish adding the beads and lace in good time for you to get ready. I can't wait to see you and Miss Annabel in all your finery." Molly carefully helped undo the tiny buttons at the back of the dress, treating it with the utmost respect, just as Mrs Pratt had told her to.

JUST AS PENNY was going downstairs to lunch, there was a sharp rap at the door. "I'll get it, Mr Plummer," she called. The butler's arthritis always played up in cold, wet weather, and she hurried across the ornately tiled entrance hall to see who it was.

"Penny, I hope you don't mind me calling unannounced. I was passing, and it seemed like too good an opportunity to miss." The tall man at the top of the steps took his hat off and brushed the raindrops from his riding cape.

"Hello, Great Uncle Edmund." Penny opened the door wider to let him in.

Edmund Calder's eyes narrowed as he watched one of the stable boys lead his prancing stallion away. "Give him a good rub down, and mind you handle him properly," he called sharply. He rolled his eyes as he turned back to Penny. "That horse cost me a pretty penny. I hope the boy's up to looking after him."

She bit back a sigh. "I can vouch for all the staff being more than capable of doing the jobs Grand-papa employs them to do."

"Of course, although I always think that Henry is far too soft with his servants. They need to know their place, otherwise, they have a habit of getting above themselves, which is no good to anyone." Edmund took his riding cape off without being asked, thrusting it towards Mr Plummer with a disdainful look, and Penny darted an apologetic smile in the butler's direction.

"Are you here to see the master?" Plummer asked. His face was impassive, but Penny knew from the slight twitch of his bushy eyebrows that he was annoyed at the way Sir Henry's brother treated Talbot Manor as though he owned the place.

Edmund sniffed the air. With his mutton-chop whiskers, the gesture reminded Penny of an over-eager bloodhound, and she coughed to cover the sudden urge to laugh. "It smells as though I'm just in time for luncheon. I'm sure Mrs Pratt won't mind laying the table for one more person."

"Edmund, my dear. This is a lovely surprise." Juliet's silk gown rustled as she glided towards her brother-in-law with a broad smile. "Henry is feeling unwell and has taken to his bed." She pouted prettily and linked arms with him. "You know I hate eating luncheon alone, so you must join us. I want to hear all your news from London...everything is still as dull as ever here on the estate, and I'm tired of listening to Henry droning on about social reform."

Mrs Pratt pursed her lips with irritation as she bustled past. "Why does she say she's eating alone when you and Miss Annabel and Master Oscar are here to keep her company?" she muttered to Penny. "It ain't right the way she comments about Sir Henry, either; it's not as if he's poorly on purpose."

Penny could only shrug, although secretly, she agreed with the way Plummer and Mrs Pratt felt about her grandfather's brother. Barely a week went by without Edmund Calder finding some reason or other to call in, and he had an annoying way of making subtle digs about Henry, as though he had come by owning Talbot Manor through idle good fortune instead of years of hard work, building his importing business.

Only last week, Penny had overheard Mrs Pratt and Daphne talking in the kitchen about him.

"He was always jealous of Sir Henry," Mrs Pratt had said darkly. "He likes to tell everyone that the master was lucky to buy the manor, even though it's not true."

"Exactly," Daphne had agreed. "I've never cooked for anyone who works as hard as Sir Henry, even when he was grieving after Miss Louisa left and Lady Helen passed away. Just because Edmund is a solicitor, he thinks he's so superior to everyone, although I've heard whispers in town that he ain't even a very good solicitor."

"You don't have to tell me, Daphne. You don't know the half of it." Elsie Pratt's low mutterings had sounded outraged. "Some folk even say that he took on all manner of shady deals after his wife died because he had terrible gambling debts. If you ask me, the poor woman was better off out of it; God rest her soul."

"Mama! Penny has agreed to come to the ball with us." Annabel's excited cry as she ran down the stairs snapped Penny back to the present.

"It's mainly just to keep Oscar company," Penny said hastily as she saw Juliet frown. "I can fetch drinks for him and fend people off if there are too many questions about his injury."

"I suppose I don't mind…as long as you don't steal the limelight from Annabel. I have high hopes for Benedict and her, and I don't want you ruining the night with your earnest conversations, Penny. You can be as tedious as your grandfather in that respect."

Penny felt her cheeks burn at the dismissive way that Juliet had spoken to her.

"Don't worry, she doesn't mean it," Oscar whispered as he sat down stiffly next to her at the dinner table. "I find our conversations quite entertaining."

"What's this about a ball?" Edmund asked, giving Juliet an innocent smile. "Do you mean the one Sir Peregrine Walker is holding?"

"Yes. I've been looking forward to it for weeks, but Henry has decided not to go, which means I can't go either." Juliet pouted again, toying with the soup that Molly had just served.

"Whyever not? Just because Henry is turning into a miserable old hermit doesn't mean you should have to while away your days in isolation, Juliet." Edmund glanced at Oscar and raised his eyebrows. "Why don't I take Henry's place? I know Peregrine well, and I'm sure he won't mind. Your mama deserves to enjoy herself, don't you think, Oscar?"

"Won't that set tongues wagging?" Annabel looked alarmed. She needed everything to be perfect, and Edmund was much younger than his brother Henry. The last thing she wanted was the whiff of any impropriety that might make Benedict think the Calders were not a good family to marry into.

"Really, Annabel, you can be very selfish at times," Juliet said sulkily. "What could be more proper than Edmund stepping in to help his brother's family? I've known Edmund for years…it was he who introduced me to Sir Henry, if you recall. It's not as if anyone is going to think we're doing something wrong."

"I can ask Sir Henry if that's what you want," Edmund said, giving Annabel an amused look, "although I hardly think it's necessary to disturb the poor fellow on his sickbed. I shall merely act as chaperone to take the burden from Oscar."

"It's fine…I just don't want to stir up any gossip," Annabel said quietly.

Penny felt rather sorry for her. As much as Annabel enjoyed being the centre of attention at home, whenever they were in company, Penny noticed that Juliet liked to make sure that all eyes were on her, as if she was worried that her own daughter might outshine her.

"Well, that's all settled then." Juliet gave Edmund a bright smile. "I have a new gown for the occasion and something to look forward to, at long last. I don't know how we would manage without your thoughtfulness, Edmund. Your company is a real tonic."

"Poor Henry won't know what he's missing out on," Edmund replied, resting his hand momentarily over Juliet's. "I trust you will do me the great honour of giving me the first dance?"

Juliet looked coy, not noticing the worried glance that Oscar and Annabel had exchanged. "Of course, Edmund. It will be just like old times before Sir Henry stole my heart. Do you remember the evening when you introduced us…it was the winter ball at Claridge's."

As Penny listened to Juliet and Edmund reminiscing, she found herself drawn into the entertaining stories about some of Edmund's clients. Most appeared to be larger-than-life characters who operated with scant regard for the law as long as there was a good time to be had or money to be made. He was very different from Henry, who only liked to work with people who he deemed to be decent and trustworthy.

Edmund seemed unusually talkative, and she wasn't sure whether it was because of the good claret he had told Molly to fetch from Henry's cellar or the fact that Henry was unwell and in bed, giving him more license to chat freely with Juliet. Either way, Juliet hung on every word, laughing gaily at his jokes and nodding along in a way she rarely did when Henry ate luncheon with them.

But what surprised Penny more than how well they were getting along was how long they had known each other. She had always assumed that Edmund had just been an acquaintance of Juliet's who had introduced her to his brother, Sir Henry. But instead, it seemed that Edmund had known Juliet for a number of years before the introduction. He had even helped her get the position as a companion to one of his late client's wives when she was widowed. She wondered idly whether Juliet had ever had romantic feelings towards Edmund but then quickly pushed the thought to one side because it felt too disloyal to her grandfather. Henry had provided a good life for Juliet, and no expense had been spared to take care of Oscar and Annabel as well. Plus, she knew that her grandfather loved Juliet in his own quiet way. Penny just hoped that Juliet appreciated it.

CHAPTER 14

"What do you mean Mama has already gone?" Annabel practically stamped her foot with annoyance as they assembled in the entrance hall.

"I'm sorry, Miss Annabel, but I'm just passing on the message." Plummer was used to Annabel's outbursts, and he knew her temper was not really directed at him. "While you were upstairs getting ready, Mr Calder returned with his brougham, which, as you know, only seats two people."

"But she was meant to travel with us so we would all arrive together." Annabel looked close to tears, and Penny laid a hand on her arm to comfort her.

"Mama was complaining about how rough our carriage was the last time we went into town, don't you remember?" Oscar was looking very dashing, but it was lost on Annabel. "Also, as Edmund was leaving after luncheon, I overheard him telling Mama that his brougham would be far more comfortable for her."

"But what are people going to think if they arrive together, leaving us trailing behind like the poor relations?"

"Hush, Miss Annabel. You don't want to spoil your looks by getting yourself in a tizzy." Mrs Pratt adjusted the silk shawl over Annabel's shoulders and stood back to admire her and Penny.

"Don't you both look beautiful," Molly said, clasping her hands together with tears of happiness in her eyes. At the sight of the two young women dressed in all their finery, even Mr Plummer was clearing his throat with emotion.

Daphne wiped her hands on her apron and rushed forward to kiss Penny. "You look so much like Louisa, it's brought a lump to my throat. And you're a vision of loveliness, Annabel. I only wish Sir Henry was well enough to come downstairs and see you both."

"We went to his bedroom to say farewell, but he was asleep," Penny said. "Will you make sure his room is kept nice and warm this evening?"

"Come along," Oscar said, tapping his walking stick with a mischievous smile. "You know Plummer and Mrs Pratt have everything in hand. The gentlemen at the ball will be lining up to fill your dance cards, and we mustn't keep them waiting.

Annabel gave everyone a gracious smile, her good humour restored. "We'll tell you all about it tomorrow, every last detail."

"I'm sure the food won't be a scratch on yours, Daphne," Oscar said. The cook's cheeks turned pink, but she was saved from further blushes by the arrival of the carriage at the bottom of the steps.

Mr Webster climbed down from his seat and opened the door. "It looks like the rain is holding off, for now, miss," he said as Annabel hurried out. "I'll have you there in no time, and Mrs Webster has put some rugs in the carriage to keep you warm."

Annabel sighed happily as they settled back against the leather squabs, glad to be on their way.

"Look, Grandfather is at the window." Penny fluttered her handkerchief to wave goodbye as she saw him watching from above. He looked frail in his dressing gown, and his shock of white hair gave her a moment of sadness. He had been such a steady presence in Penny's life for the last few years that it was hard to see the vitality leaching out of him because of ill health, and she couldn't imagine life at Talbot Manor without Sir Henry at the head of the family.

They were soon bowling along the country lanes towards Sir Peregrine's estate, and Annabel was in high spirits. "Do you think Benedict will enjoy being out of London?" she mused. "And what about you, Oscar? Have you thought about what you might do now that the Royal Artillery is no longer an option?"

Oscar rubbed his aching leg as he considered his sister's question. "I was hoping that there might be some sort of job for me still within the Artillery, but not in active fighting."

"Is the doctor pleased with your recovery?" Penny hadn't liked to pry, but he seemed more willing to talk about it now. "It might be hard to take a sedentary role after leading your men into battle."

"I've thought about that," Oscar said with a rueful smile. "The doctor said that if I push myself, there's no reason why I can't ride a horse again at some point, and the limp will become less pronounced. Also, he said not to make any hasty decisions about my career, so I'm taking his advice for the time being."

"Well, we like having you home again," Annabel said. "Mama has been so distracted lately. Goodness knows what she has on her mind, but between that and Penny helping Sir Henry with more of his work, I've been left at a loose end."

"It sounds like it's high time for you to be courting a nice young man." Oscar chuckled, knowing that this was exactly what his sister had in mind. "I've made a few discreet enquiries, and Benedict Walker would make a good match for you."

"I don't need your seal of approval," Annabel replied sniffily. Her curiosity was piqued nonetheless. "What do you know about him?" she continued a moment later.

"He was well regarded in business circles when he was managing Sir Peregrine's affairs in London since he became a Member of Parliament. And from what I could tell, he seems an honourable sort of fellow."

Penny was happy to see a look of relief in Annabel's eyes. The rumours of a few dalliances ending in heartbreak must have been just that. She knew that Oscar would not speak highly of someone interested in his sister if he thought they'd behaved like a cad in the past.

Since leaving Talbot Manor, the heavens had opened again, and it was hard to make themselves heard with the drumming of rain on the roof of the carriage. The lanes quickly turned to mud, and they could hear Webster's calls of encouragement urging the horses onward, even though it was slow going.

"Mama was right about this carriage," Annabel grumbled. She grabbed the door handle as it juddered over a particularly rough bit of ground. "I shall look completely dishevelled by the time we arrive."

"Don't be silly, Annabel," Oscar sighed. "You're warm and dry, and a few bumps along the way aren't going to harm you."

Before Annabel could reply, the carriage suddenly lurched violently, and the horses whinnied with fear.

"You see…we'll be lucky to arrive in one piece," Annable shrieked, clutching her shawl. She peered out of the window into the darkness. "Why have we stopped?"

A moment later, Percy Webster's face loomed at the window. He opened the carriage door a crack, standing in the gap so as not to let the scything rain in. "Don't panic. It looks like one of the traces on the carriage has partially snapped, but I'll have it mended in no time."

"I must help you," Oscar said, looking worried. He tried to struggle to his feet.

"Certainly not, sir. I won't hear of it." The rain was running down Mr Webster's face in rivulets, but he shook his head firmly. "It's just a minor repair, and I can lash it together with some rope… although perhaps you could persuade Sir Henry to consider getting a more modern carriage for the future," he added.

Annabel plucked at the corner of her shawl fretfully as the minutes passed. "What if Benedict thinks we've changed our minds and that we're not coming because of the terrible weather? He'll spend all night dancing with the other young ladies, and one of them is bound to catch his eye.

Everything is going wrong," she cried, throwing up her hands in despair and blinking back tears.

"We left home in good time," Penny said, patting Annabel's arm soothingly. "Percy is doing his best, and if Benedict's affections were so easily distracted, then he wouldn't have been right for you anyway."

Annabel sighed loudly and looked at the carriage door as though she was considering jumping out to help get the repair done faster. "It's so unfair. This is all Mama's fault," she muttered after a couple more minutes had passed.

"How so?" Oscar asked.

"I don't know," Annabel said crossly. "It just feels as though she's too busy entertaining Edmund lately to pay attention to running the estate. It's too much for Henry to do when he's feeling ill, and Edmund could have offered to take us all in his larger carriage instead of taking only her in that brougham. It's ridiculous...he's showing off without a care for the rest of us."

Penny couldn't help but agree, although she didn't say it out loud. Edmund's visits had become more frequent since Sir Henry had become ill. Every time he came, he said it was to visit his brother, but he rarely spent more than a few minutes with him before finding a reason to seek out Juliet instead.

"I'll speak to Sir Henry about whether we can get a better carriage in the next few days," Oscar said, trying to calm Annabel. "Now that I'm feeling better, perhaps I should take on more of the work managing the estate. I know you help your grandfather with his letters and the like, Penny, but I'm sure I could do more if you think he'll agree?"

Just as she was about to nod, Percy opened the carriage door again and leaned in. "I've done enough to get you all to the ball and home again." He grimaced, looking like a drowned rat as a fresh deluge of rain fell from the sky.

"Thank you so much, Percy," Penny said hastily before Annabel could complain again about them being late.

A cough rattled in the coachman's chest, and he pulled his collar up before slamming the door closed again.

"I feel guilty that the poor fellow is drenched," Oscar said with a frown. "I hope he's not going to catch a chill."

"I'm more worried about us getting soaked walking from the carriage into the ball," Annabel muttered. She shivered and tucked the rug tighter over her knees as the horses trotted smartly on again.

The fickle weather had changed again as they arrived at Sir Peregrine Walker's country estate, Blaenwen Hall. Flaming torches lit the way, dotted along the side of the carriage sweep, and Penny was relieved to see that there were several carriages drawing up behind them. They were not the last to arrive, which lifted Annabel's mood instantly.

A liveried footman crunched across the gravel and doffed his hat as he helped them all alight. The doors at the top of the steps had been thrown open, and there were swags of autumn foliage framing the entrance.

"Annabel, I was beginning to worry that you weren't coming." Benedict Walker bounded down the steps to welcome them.

"I wouldn't have missed it for the world," she replied with a tinkling laugh. The sound of music drifted out from the ballroom, and Annabel positively glowed with happiness as Benedict tucked her gloved hand into the crook of his arm.

"Come and meet my parents," he said, smiling at Penny and Oscar to include them too. He leaned closer to Annabel. "I'm very glad you're here. Some of the young ladies Mama invited from London are determined to make me dance with them, but I told her you are my favourite guest tonight. Please agree to dance with me, Annabel…if only to save me from all the inane chit-chat of those other ladies."

Penny and Oscar exchanged a relieved glance as Annabel flushed prettily at Benedict's effusive welcome and smiled up at him with a gracious nod. Her iridescent blue gown matched her eyes perfectly, and Penny thought they made a striking couple as they glided up the steps together. She felt herself starting to relax after the stresses of their journey, but it was short-lived as she saw Mr Webster clutching the carriage, gasping as another coughing fit consumed him.

"I think we should send Mr Webster home, Oscar, don't you? The poor fellow looks awful, and I would feel terribly guilty if he got ill on our account." Without waiting for an answer, she turned back.

"Percy, you must go home. I don't want you waiting up until the small hours for us, or you'll catch a chill."

The elderly coachman shook his head stubbornly. "I know you mean well, Miss Penny, but I don't like letting Sir Henry down. I'm the head coachman, and it's my job to drive the carriage." His eyes looked suspiciously bright, and he suddenly pulled his handkerchief out to catch three sneezes.

"You won't be letting anyone down," Penny said firmly. "Take the carriage home, and send one of the other stable boys in your place. I'm sure they can handle the horses just fine." She sensed his resolve was weakening and gave him a kind smile. "What would Abigail say if she knew you were standing out here for hours, soaked to the skin? You need a nice hot toddy by the fire and a mustard compress on your chest. Maude used to swear by that for coughs and colds."

Percy's expression brightened at the thought of being back in his cosy cottage with Abigail taking care of him. "If you're sure, miss? Young Wilfred is a careful driver, and I'll be sure to send him back in good time."

Penny nodded, and a moment later, Oscar placed her hand on his arm. "Time for us to enjoy the ball?" he asked with a grin.

. . .

THE SPACIOUS ENTRANCE hall of Blaenwen Hall was ablaze with dozens of tall candles, and the air was heady with the scent of lilies and roses, which were artistically arranged in silver urns and cut glass vases giving the grand house a sense of lushness and decadence.

"Welcome," Sir Peregrine called from the entrance to the ballroom. "I'm glad you were able to come, Oscar. Good to see that you're on the mend. Benedict told me it was a nasty wound, but I'm sure you gave the enemy what for."

Oscar murmured a reply and was grateful for Penny's tact as she turned the conversation to how lovely the ballroom looked.

"It's all down to my wife," Peregrine said cheerfully. "I can't claim to have an artistic bone in my body...give me a day in Parliament instead, any time. Now, you must go and enjoy the music, even if you're not quite up to dancing yet, Oscar. I'm sure Miss Calder won't be short of dance partners in that charming red gown. You look every bit as beautiful as your mother was at your age."

Penny and Oscar chose a table at the edge of the room where they had a good view of the other guests who were already swirling around the floor in a lively polka. Oscar lifted his hand to attract the attention of one of the servants, who brought them two glasses of fruit punch.

"I don't think I've ever seen Annabel look so happy," Penny commented as she spotted her in Benedict's arms, being skillfully guided around the dancefloor. Annabel's cheeks were rosy as they twirled past, and Benedict's head was tilted towards her as they talked.

"He certainly seems to have eyes for nobody but her," Oscar commented drily. His face clouded as the dancers parted for a moment, and he spotted his mother and Edmund on the far side of the room. "I hope Edmund doesn't drink too much," he muttered. "He can be rather careless in his behaviour when he does, and I don't want Mama's reputation brought into question."

Penny followed Oscar's gaze and felt a shiver of alarm. Juliet's gaze was rapt as she listened to Edmund telling one of his stories, and even from this distance, she could see that it was a look of more than mere friendship. It confirmed her worst suspicions, and worry gnawed in the pit of her stomach. It seemed as though Juliet was growing weary of the inevitable frailties of her much older husband and was seeking attention from Edmund instead.

"I'm sure they won't do anything untoward," she said hastily. "Edmund has clients here; I expect he's just being friendly to make up for Grandpapa not being able to come with us." She hoped that Annabel would be too taken up with Benedict's company to notice because even though the girl could be self-absorbed, Penny knew she was very fond of her stepfather.

"May I interrupt you to ask for the next dance?" A tall gentleman bowed courteously in front of Penny and shot an enquiring look in Oscar's direction. "I'm Benedict's cousin, Arthur Sinclair," he explained. "Uncle Peregrine said that you're recovering from an injury, and it would be a shame for your charming companion not to enjoy some of the dances, don't you think?"

Oscar shook hands with him and nodded enthusiastically. "As long as you take good care of her. I have two left feet when it comes to ballroom dancing anyway, so it's a good thing I'm sitting out."

Penny rose gracefully from her seat just as the orchestra started the first bars of a Viennese waltz. She was grateful that it was a dance she knew.

"I'll be back shortly to check that you're alright," she said to Oscar, but he waved her away.

Penny was oblivious to admiring glances from some of the other guests as Arthur took her hand, and they started gliding around the polished floor. The ruby red gown fitted her like a glove, and her dark curls were swept into a chignon with ringlets framing her face, which showed off her elegant neck.

Arthur was an attentive dance partner, and Penny ended up staying with him for several dances before another gentleman took his place. She felt as though she was in heaven. Her feet barely touched the floor as the waltz was followed by a two-step and then a mazurka. The chandeliers sparkled overhead, and the soft light of the candles made the jewels and sequins glitter on the ladies' outfits like a thousand twinkling stars. She had never had such an enjoyable evening in her whole life and finally understood why Annabel had been so eager for her to come too.

By the time the next dance came to an end, Penny was ready for a rest, and she sat down next to Oscar again. She noticed a young lady hovering nearby, glancing shyly in their direction every now and again.

"Would you care to join us?" Penny asked, gesturing at Annabel's empty seat.

Oscar struggled to his feet and bowed. "Miss Appleby? Goodness me, I haven't seen you since I was in London last year. How do you know the Walkers?"

"My Papa works for Mr Walker and his father, managing one of the family's businesses in London." She gave Penny a nervous smile. "I was worried about coming to the ball because we don't know anyone, but Sir Peregrine likes to invite his staff to these sorts of events; he's very kind like that."

"Well, you know me," Oscar replied. A servant passed, and he asked for three new cups of fruit punch for them. "And this is Penny…Miss Calder…Sir Henry's granddaughter. So now you know two people," he added.

Penny smiled to herself as Mary Appleby and Oscar were soon talking non-stop about various mutual acquaintances. She seemed like an uncomplicated young woman who was sensitive and kind in the way she didn't pry into Oscar's injuries sustained in battle, which endeared her even more to Penny.

"You must come and visit us at Talbot Manor if you and your papa are staying here for a while," she said on the spur of the moment when there was a lull in the music.

"Indeed you must," Oscar agreed. "I can show you the orangery...I seem to remember in London that you said you like exotic flowers. The gardeners have all sorts of orchids and plants from Sir Henry's travels overseas that I think you would enjoy."

"I'm going to get some fresh air." Penny searched the dancefloor and saw that Annabel and Benedict were still gliding around to a slow waltz, and suddenly she felt rather like a spare part. She had hoped that Arthur would accompany her, but he was deep in conversation with two gentlemen, so she decided to slip out by herself to cool down and also to give Oscar and Mary some time together.

Penny was surprised to see the yellow glow of a full moon just rising as she strolled out into the formal rose garden, which was just beyond the ballroom. There were torches burning at various points near the house, and the rain had long since blown away, leaving ragged clouds which scudded across the sky.

After the heat of the ballroom and the hum of chatter, it was a relief to be in the cool night air.

An owl hooted in the distance, followed a moment later by the bark of a vixen out hunting. She walked towards the end of the garden between the low box hedges, enjoying the peace and quiet, but suddenly the sound of muffled laughter drifted towards her, followed by whispers.

"...Edmund...tell me again..."

Penny froze. It was Juliet's voice.

"You're the most beautiful woman there this evening, Juliet...you know how I feel..."

The clouds which had momentarily covered the moon drifted away, and Penny gasped as she saw Edmund and Juliet silhouetted in a passionate embrace. She felt anger rising up inside her at the scandal which would erupt if anyone else saw them. It would ruin Annabel's chances with Benedict and cast her grandfather as a cuckold, but Juliet didn't seem to care.

As soon as a cloud covered the moon again, Penny hurried back into the ballroom. All she could do was put it out of her mind and hope that it was just a lapse of manners brought on by the intimacy of an evening spent dancing and perhaps too many glasses of punch.

Thankfully, Oscar and Mary were still enjoying each other's company, and before Penny had a chance to brood on what she had just witnessed, Arthur asked her to dance again.

The rest of the evening passed by in a flash. There was a sumptuous meal, followed by more dancing, and then, as the clock struck one, it was time to leave.

"I think this was the best evening of my life," Annabel said dreamily as Benedict escorted them outside.

"I would like to call as soon as possible," he said, gazing meaningfully into her eyes.

"Perhaps you could bring Miss Appleby over in a few days and come together?" Oscar suggested.

"It looks like the evening has been a great success for Annabel and Oscar," Arthur commented as he tucked Penny's hand in the crook of his arm. "I sense love could be in the air for both of them, thanks to Uncle Peregrine's generous hospitality."

Penny nodded with a warm glow of contentment in her chest. In spite of seeing Juliet and Edmund in the garden, she was happy that Oscar and Mary had hit it off so well and even more delighted that Annabel and Benedict had spent practically the whole evening together dancing.

"What about you, Miss Calder...or may I call

you Penny?" Arthur said softly. "You have made the evening far more enjoyable than I thought it would be."

Penny blushed. She hadn't given much thought to courting, preferring to help her grandfather with his work, but Arthur seemed kind, and she had enjoyed his company. "I had a wonderful evening, too," she said. She wasn't as practised at fielding compliments as Annabel and didn't know what to say next. "That's our carriage. I'd better go; I don't want to keep the others waiting."

Arthur bent over and brushed a kiss on the back of Penny's gloved hand. "Perhaps I could ride over to visit you for tea soon?"

Just as Penny was about to reply, their carriage drew up at the bottom of the steps, and she could scarcely believe her eyes at who jumped down from the driver's seat to open the door for Annabel.

"George?" she cried.

He looked up at Penny, and his eyes widened with surprise at the sight of how beautiful she looked. He hastily recovered his composure and tipped his hat, giving her a wide smile.

"Percy sent for me," he explained. "Wilfred, the stable boy, wasn't paying attention, and one of the horses kicked him. Abigail had to put him to bed until the doctor can come to make sure there are no broken bones."

Penny flushed as his warm brown eyes crinkled with the smile she knew so well. "Thank goodness you were able to step in and help."

George's gaze lingered appreciatively on Penny, taking in the ballgown and the sparkling jewels at her neck. He had never seen her look so elegant, and it practically took his breath away.

Arthur coughed discreetly and stepped back. "Send me a note to let me know when it might be convenient to visit, Miss Calder…if that's what you would like?"

"Yes…yes, of course, that would be lovely," Penny stuttered, looking between the two men.

A moment later, George handed her into the carriage. "It's nice to see you again," he murmured in a low voice. "I barely recognised you."

"It's been too long," Penny replied softly. Although she tried to visit Sketty Lane whenever she could, helping her grandpapa with his work had taken up so much of her time that the weeks had slipped by, and it had been months since her last visit. She felt a sudden pang of regret and hoped that he didn't think she had turned her back on her past.

"I expect you've just been busy with your new life…which is as it should be. You look beautiful, like a proper lady." George's expression was hard to read, but Penny felt her heart skip a beat at the light pressure of his hand on her arm and, with it, the familiar surge of tumultuous emotions she always felt in his company.

CHAPTER 15

"Mrs Fraser has made your favourite, Grandpapa. Shall I sit with you while you eat it?" Penny bustled into Sir Henry's bedroom with a steaming bowl of chicken broth and bread rolls, which had come fresh out of the range just half an hour earlier. The aroma of the food was making her mouth water, and she hoped it would tempt him to eat.

Henry tightened the belt of his dressing gown and hobbled slowly from his bed to the table in the window. A fire crackled in the grate, releasing a pleasing scent of fragrant applewood, and the room felt cosy compared to the grey winter's day outside.

"I should be downstairs, really; I just can't seem

to shake this wretched cold off." Henry coughed wheezily as he sat down. "I don't like putting Cook to any trouble."

"Don't be silly, Grandpapa. You know Daphne's never happier than when she's cooking special dishes to help people get better. Now that Oscar is back to full health, she can concentrate on you." Penny chuckled. "She's even been sending meals over to the cottage for Mr Webster...you can imagine what Abigail had to say about that."

Henry took a spoonful of the aromatic broth and sighed appreciatively while Penny slathered some golden butter onto the bread rolls. It was churned freshly every week from their own herd of milking cows, which she knew he liked.

"I've been very lucky to have such loyal servants over the years," he mused. "How is young Wilfred? Is his leg on the mend?"

"Luck has nothing to do with it," Penny countered. "It's because you're a kind employer." She threw another log onto the fire, and a shower of sparks flew up the chimney. Even though she found the room hot, it didn't take much for Henry to start shivering again. "The doctor said that as long as Wilfred doesn't overdo it, his broken leg will heal nicely. It's fortunate that he's still young;

otherwise, it could have been worse. Of course, he's itching to get back to work, so George is giving him easy jobs he can do sitting down, cleaning the tack and suchlike."

"And what about Percy Webster? Mrs Pratt said he looked dreadful when he returned home on the night of the ball."

Penny's brow furrowed with guilt. "The pneumonia is lingering, Grandpapa. It's probably not just from that night, although I do feel bad that he got so wet. But you know he'd been finding the winters hard for the last few years. Abigail is nursing him, but it's taking a while for him to get better."

"It seems we're none of us getting any younger," Henry said with a wry smile. He gave his granddaughter a shrewd look, noticing the faint pink flush on her cheeks when she mentioned George's name. He didn't think it was just from the heat of the fire.

"Maybe it's time for us older folk to start thinking about stepping back a bit, although I'm not sure what I would do if I didn't have work to fill my days."

"I hope you haven't been doing too much." Penny's tone held the hint of a scolding, but she tempered it with a smile. The sheaf of papers on the bed told her everything she needed to know, but she couldn't deny him when he asked her to fetch work from his study to keep his mind occupied.

"I just like to make sure I'm abreast of everything," he said innocently. "I've been thinking about Mr Webster. It's time for him to retire, and although I know he'll resist the idea, Abigail will persuade him, I'm sure. I shall give them a suitable allowance, and they can stay in the cottage because he has served me loyally for many years."

Penny nodded. "Not to mention reuniting me with you, Grandpapa." She had never told him about the way it had happened, and after this long, it was water under the bridge. Abigail and Percy were always polite to Penny, and she figured they probably regretted the way she had been bundled into the cart and held at the warehouse. "Would you like me to tell them?"

Henry sat back in his chair, leaving the broth only half eaten. His face was grey with tiredness, and he nodded wearily. "If you don't mind taking care of it, I'd be very grateful." He summoned a smile which made his eyes twinkle. "Of course, that leaves the small matter of who will take Percy's place as head coachman..."

Penny stood up and busied herself with putting away some freshly laundered nightclothes, not quite meeting his gaze.

"I would like you to tell George that the job is his if he would like it. I've heard he's done well, standing in for Percy while he's been ill, so we may as well make it a formal arrangement. He'll have more money, and I'd like to offer him the other cottage next to the stable block. It's small, but it will do until he ever decides to get married..."

Penny blushed at his final sentence, and Sir Henry smiled to himself. It seemed his instincts were correct.

"He'll be delighted, Grandpapa," Penny said happily once she had recovered her composure. "It's everything he's ever wanted." She gathered up the plates and sat down again. "He showed me around the stables at Melbury House once...I've never told you this."

Henry looked at her curiously and nodded to encourage her to continue the story.

"He sounded so knowledgeable about the horses...I really believe he would be good at breeding new bloodlines. Do you think that would be something good for the estate, Grandpapa? Calder horses…we could sell them to wealthy people." She hesitated, realising that she had allowed herself to run away with the idea which had been brewing ever since George had moved to Talbot Manor after the ball.

Henry patted her hand and chuckled. "I've been hoping you might suggest such a thing. I can tell you have a keen brain, Penny, which is why I've had you helping me with the business. And Mrs Pratt and Plummer tell me that George is hard-working, with plenty of ambition, as well as being loyal. I admire that in a young man."

She flushed with pleasure at his words. She should have known that even though he was stuck in his bedroom, he still had his finger on the pulse of what was happening on the estate. That was her Grandpapa's way. "I'll tell him later today. He'll be so grateful that you're giving him this opportunity."

"You'd better go and have some luncheon of your own now. Otherwise, Mrs Pratt will tell me off for making you work too hard." Henry hobbled over to the wingback armchair next to the fire, where he would enjoy an afternoon nap. "Perhaps Juliet might come upstairs and read to me later?" he asked hopefully as Penny was leaving.

"I'll suggest it to her," Penny replied, closing the door softly.

* * *

"I DON'T THINK I'll have time," Juliet said a little while later as they were having luncheon. She gestured for Molly to remove the plates and serve dessert. "I don't like being cooped up in his bedroom, to be honest. It's too hot, and I worry about whether his ailments might be contagious." Her tone was peevish, and she looked irritated that Penny had suggested she could go and read to Henry in front of Oscar and Annabel.

"What are you so busy with, Mama?" Annabel asked curiously. "Poor Sir Henry hardly sees you these days, and it can't be much fun for him having to stay indoors."

"You'd be surprised how demanding it is running this place," Juliet countered quickly.

Oscar raised his eyebrows at the over-exaggeration. As far as he knew, Penny was running the household staff singlehandedly, as well as helping with Henry's business matters, and he was taking care of many of the decisions to do with the estate and farm.

"I have letters to write, and my dressmaker is coming later on today for a fitting," Juliet explained with an extravagant sigh. "Edmund has very kindly invited me to the theatre this evening with some of his business acquaintances."

Annabel's face fell with disappointment. "Did you forget that Benedict is coming to have tea with me this afternoon? I've been looking forward to it for days, and you promised you would be there too." She crossed her arms and sat back, not touching the egg custard Molly had just put in front of her.

"Edmund does seem to be spending rather a lot of time in your company, Mama," Oscar said carefully. "Sir Peregrine commented about it when I saw him last week."

Juliet threw down her linen napkin and stood up abruptly. "I will not be told how to conduct myself by you three," she snapped, including Penny in her indignant glare of disapproval. "Do you have any idea how hard it is for me, stuck in this draughty manor house day after day with nothing to look forward to? Henry is practically at death's door, and Edmund is just being kind."

"I don't think Grandpapa is that bad," Penny muttered. She lifted her chin defiantly. "We're doing our best to get him well again. All he wants is some time in your company. Is that too much to ask?"

"You're getting above yourself, young lady," Juliet cried, pointing a trembling finger at Penny. "I've put up with you all these years to keep Henry happy, but things will change after he's gone."

Annabel gasped at her mother's cruel words. "Mama! Penny has every right to be here. She's Henry's granddaughter, for goodness sake."

"That was a thoughtless thing to say," Oscar added, agreeing with Annabel.

Juliet pressed a hand to her brow. "You're bringing on one of my headaches with your comments. Edmund is the only person who shows me any kindness, so I shall go to the theatre if I want to." She swept towards the door, making Molly scurry to get out of her way. "I'm head of Talbot Manor, second to your grandfather, and you'd do well to remember it," Juliet said as she left, giving Penny a stern look.

Oscar looked embarrassed at his mother's behaviour, and Annabel blinked back tears.

"What is Benedict going to think about all this? I can't take tea with him without a chaperone."

"Don't worry, Penny or I can do it instead," Oscar said good-naturedly. "Besides, Mrs Pratt will probably be hovering nearby, ready to ply him with more cake. You know she's hoping you'll be announcing an engagement soon, now that you're courting properly."

Annabel smiled at her brother. He always knew how to cheer her up when their mother was in one of her moods. "Speaking of courting, how is the delightful Mary Appleby? Is she coming down from London again?"

"The gardeners said she was very taken with your tour of the orangery and the flowers you gave her," Penny added, grinning as Oscar turned red.

"We've been exchanging letters, if you must know," he confessed. "She's very entertaining and doesn't witter on about fashion and other boring things.

Annabel clapped her hands together. "I knew as soon as Penny told me you spent most of the evening at the ball talking to her that she would be perfect for you, Oscar. Maybe we'll have two spring weddings to look forward to?" she added with a coy smile.

Penny excused herself, leaving Annabel and Oscar to discuss how their respective romances were progressing, eager to pass on her grandfather's message to George. She tied a woollen cloak over her shoulders and went to the kitchen to get some cake to take out for Wilfred.

"That boy's got the appetite of a horse," Daphne declared, cutting a thick slab of fruitcake for him. She wrapped it in a cloth and reached for a basket, adding some bread and cheese for good measure.

"I believe Lady Calder will be dining out this evening," Penny said.

Mrs Pratt harrumphed, looking up from her menu plan, and exchanged a dark look with Daphne. "Yes, we know. Out again with Sir Henry's brother, I fancy," she muttered.

Penny didn't want to encourage gossip, so she changed the subject hastily. "Do you need any help preparing tea for Benedict Walker's visit? Annabel wants it to be perfect."

"Leave it to us, miss." Daphne shooed her away. "I'll be making dainty cucumber sandwiches, and I've just finished making them fancy little cakes Miss Annabel is so fond of. Besides, you're not meant to work in the kitchen with the likes of us, it ain't right."

"Old habits die hard," Penny chuckled, beating a hasty retreat. She knew full well Daphne would provide a sumptuous spread. It was a matter of household pride to outshine the cook at Blaenwen Hall, plus they were all eagerly hoping that Benedict would propose to Annabel soon.

THE COMFORTING sweet smell of hay tickled Penny's nose as she entered the large barn where the horses were stabled, and Wilfred grinned at her from the corner where he was busy buffing dubbin on one of her side saddles.

"Afternoon, miss," he called. He eyed the basket hungrily, and Penny took it to him. "I'd get up, but the doctor told me not to." He was sitting on a rickety old chair, and his leg was in a splint, propped up on a stool.

"You must do what he says then, Wilfred. I hear it's healing nicely though, so I'm sure you'll be back to full duties soon enough."

"That I will," he said stoutly. "I don't like being idle. Can yer pass on my thanks to Daphne, please, miss?" His stomach rumbled as he unwrapped the wedge of cake and started devouring it. "George is in the stall at the far end of the barn," he mumbled through a mouthful. "One of the brood mares is almost due to foal, and he don't want to be too far away in case she needs help."

Penny walked quietly past the rest of the horses, pausing to stroke a few of them. Above her head, one of the farm cats purred, trotting along the edge of the hayloft and then jumping down to land nimbly by her feet.

"She's hoping for some milk," George said, watching with amusement. The cat rushed over to him and wound itself sinuously around his ankles, and he bent down to stroke it.

"Wilfred said one of your mares is about to foal." Penny spoke quietly, not wanting to scare any of the horses, and George jerked his head towards the stall behind him.

"She's not long had it." He dunked his arms in a bucket of water and briskly scrubbed them with some lye soap. "I thought I might have to lend a hand, but she managed by herself. She's a good broodmare, and she's had a lovely little filly. Percy did well. He bought her for a song, and she should have a few more foals in the future."

Penny tiptoed over to the wooden half door, and they stood side by side, watching the foal take her first shaky steps on a bed of straw. A moment later, she was suckling under the mare's belly, and George sighed happily. "That's what I like to see. The little 'un should be fine now it's having a feed."

"You enjoy this, don't you?" Penny said softly. It was a statement more than a question.

"If I could do this for a living, along with driving the carriages for Sir Henry, I'd be a happy man," George replied.

"In that case, I have good news for you." Penny couldn't keep the excitement out of her voice any longer. "Grandpapa has decided that it's time for Percy to step back...it's too much for him being outside in all weathers, and he has served the family for many years. He would like you to take his place as head coachman, George. And not only that, I told him that I think you would do very well breeding more horses that we could sell to the toffs." She slipped back into her old way of speaking, which made George chuckle.

"That's wonderful news," he said. "And you did that for me? How can I ever thank you?" He took her hands in his and squeezed them before realising that Wilfred was watching. He let her hands go again reluctantly and gave her a warm smile.

"You deserve it, George." She wished he was still holding her hands but knew that it was inappropriate, and the last thing she wanted was for the servants to start gossiping.

"Will you be part of it, too?" he asked hesitantly. "I mean, I know you take a keen interest in the estate, and I'd like to involve you in selecting bloodlines. It's a fascinating subject, and it might pique Sir Henry's interest too when you tell him about what we're doing." He didn't need to add that having a new project to get involved in might help his recovery, but Penny knew that was what he meant.

"I'd like that very much. In fact, as soon as I leave here, I shall go and tell Grandpapa about your new foal. She can be the first one of the Calder horses, perhaps." She plucked some hay from the rack and held it out on her palm for the sturdy cob in the next stall, smiling as his whiskers tickled her hand. "I almost forgot to say...Grandpapa will be raising your pay, and he wants you to live in the small cottage at the end of the barn. It's not fitting for the head coachman to live in the rooms over the stables."

"Wait until I tell Maude about this." George whistled cheerfully as he picked up a broom to start sweeping.

"I must go and visit her soon." Penny felt a pang of guilt.

"She misses you," George said, pausing to lean on his broom. "Now that she's not working at Culpepper's anymore and Nell is married with two young children of her own, life is rather different for her. Not that Maude regrets stopping at the brickworks," he added hastily. "It was generous of Sir Henry to pay her for raising you all those years, and Nell is happy enough helping in her husband's bakery."

"I miss her as well," Penny said. "Perhaps you could drive me into Brynwell next week, and we could take her out for a ride in the carriage? She'd like that."

"Are you sure Lady Calder would approve?"

Penny tossed her curls in a flash of defiance. "It's none of her business. I can visit Maude if I want to. Grandpapa always said he owed her a great debt of gratitude, even if Juliet was a terrible snob towards her."

Suddenly the sound of running footsteps drifted towards them, and a moment later, Molly burst into the barn and skidded to a halt by Wilfred, her mobcap all askew. "Where's Miss Penny?" she demanded breathlessly.

"Just there." Wilfred jerked his head, and Molly hastily picked her way over the straw.

"What is it?" Penny had a sense of foreboding at the panicky look on Molly's face.

"'Tis Sir Henry," she wailed. "I took him up a tray of tea and cakes, and he was wheezing something terrible, miss. I think he's taken a turn for the worse, and Mr Plummer said I was to come and fetch you immediately."

George placed his hand on Penny's shoulder and gave her a searching look. "Promise that you'll ask me if there's anything I can do to help."

"I will," she said gratefully. His straightforward nature and thoughtfulness were a stark contrast to Juliet's careless disregard for her grandfather.

"Will he be alright, Miss Penny?" Molly wrung her hands as they left together. "Talbot Manor wouldn't feel right without Sir Henry in charge."

"He's a strong man," Penny said, trying to reassure the poor girl. The sky overhead had turned slate grey, and a cold wind from the east whistled between the buildings, snatching at their skirts. "I expect he's just been overdoing things, and a few days' bedrest will do him the world of good."

Molly nodded, looking happier, and Penny sent up a silent prayer, hoping that it would be true.

CHAPTER 16

"Have I caused a panic?" Sir Henry lifted his head from the pillow and looked at Penny, who was sitting quietly by the fire. She had a book in her lap, but he could see she wasn't actually reading it.

Penny jumped up and hurried to his side. "Hush, Grandpapa. The doctor will be here shortly, but you need to rest until then."

He waved her concerns away. "He won't tell us anything we don't already know, Penny. I'm an old man, and I won't last forever. There's no point pretending otherwise. Help me sit up, will you."

Penny plumped the pillows and made her grandfather comfortable. She didn't like the sound of the wheezy rattle in his chest, and Molly was quite right; it was worse than it had been that morning.

"That's as maybe, but I won't leave your side until we know if anything more can be done to help you." She walked over to the windows to close the heavy curtains against the cold. It had started snowing outside and was settling on the frozen ground already. She hoped it wouldn't delay Doctor Grant, the family's physician.

"Did you ask Juliet if she would come up and read to me?" Henry's expression was hopeful as he glanced towards the door. "I know she's busy, but I do so enjoy her company."

Penny rattled the poker in the fire and added a couple more logs to give herself a moment to think. Edmund had arrived with his brougham carriage an hour ago, and Juliet had looked ravishing in her new dress as she glided down the stairs to meet him.

"She said she hoped you wouldn't mind her going ahead with Edmund's planned trip to the theatre, Grandpapa." She tried to keep her voice light, but a shadow clouded Henry's eyes at her answer.

"I see...I expect Edmund is entertaining clients. Poor Juliet found it hard when we moved here. I think she preferred being in London, so if an evening at the theatre keeps her spirits up, I can't deny her that bit of pleasure, and I know Edmund will take good care of her."

"Perhaps I could read to you instead?" Penny offered.

Henry shook his head and sighed. "I'm being a bit of an old fool, Penny. I've always known that Juliet married me for convenience, but I genuinely love her, you see. She was so charming and a real tonic after being alone for so long."

"I'm sure she cares a great deal about you, too, Grandpapa." Penny hoped he wouldn't be able to read her thoughts as the memory of Juliet and Edmund embracing slid into her mind.

A sudden coughing fit seized Henry and Penny felt helpless. All she could do was keep him company and hope the doctor arrived soon. After a few minutes, she held a cup of tea to his lips, and he was able to take a few sips, which seemed to revive him.

"While I have you here alone, Penny, I want to talk to you about the future of Talbot Manor."

"There's no need, Grandpapa. We'll have plenty of time to go over that when you get better. Oscar is doing a great job of looking after the estate, and

George is looking forward to showing you his plans for breeding horses."

Henry patted Penny's hand. "You're young, but you have a sensible head on your shoulders, my dear. I've been watching you blossom as you've helped me with my work, and I like the way you want to do your best to help others. You've taught me a lot."

"I would say quite the opposite," Penny replied with a self-deprecating smile. "It's you who has taught me a lot. You've been very patient explaining how things run at Talbot Manor, and I have a lot to thank you for."

Bramble had been snoozing in front of the fire, and he jumped up with one ear cocked. "That must be Doctor Grant." Before Penny could go to the door, Henry grasped her hand.

"Wait…I want to tell you what's on my mind." He paused for a moment to catch his breath. "I've left Talbot Manor to you, Penny. I know you will manage the place how I want it to be done…and there's provision for Juliet and Oscar and Annabel to be cared for, of course. They must always be able to call this their home as well."

Penny couldn't hide her shock. "But…but I thought Juliet would inherit everything?"

Henry's shoulders shuddered as another coughing fit came over him. "She doesn't love this place as you do…Penny," he gasped. "I still regret driving Louisa away…and this is my way of making up…for what I did…it's all in my will…"

Dozens of questions filled Penny's head like bees buzzing, but she knew they would have to wait when she saw the sweat beading on Henry's brow and the way he suddenly convulsed with shivers. It looked like he was getting some sort of fever, and she ran out to the upstairs landing just in time to see Doctor Grant below, taking off his greatcoat.

"Come quickly," she called down. "Grandpapa is getting worse, he needs medicine."

* * *

IT HAD BEEN A LONG NIGHT, but Penny shrugged off her tiredness as she hurried to Sir Henry's room at first light the next morning. Bramble followed her with a mournful expression. Even though he was now Penny's dog, he sensed that the master was unwell and sniffed the air warily as they entered the bedroom. It smelt of unfamiliar stringent medicines, and Penny patted the dog's head to reassure him that all was well.

"Don't worry, I've not gone yet," Henry murmured with a wry smile from the depths of his bed. A candle flickered on the mantel, and the fire was still going well, which told Penny that Molly had already been in.

"I'm glad to see it. We've had a good lot of snow overnight, Grandpapa." Penny opened the curtains so he would be able to see once it got lighter. She perched on the side of his bed and chafed his hands. His breathing still sounded laboured, but there was a bit more colour in his cheeks, much to her relief.

"Tell me what you have planned for today," he asked.

"I'm going to stay with you, of course—"

Before she could finish, Sir Henry held up one of his hands to stop her. "An old man's sick room is no place for someone your age to be sitting all day. Mrs Pratt has been popping in practically every hour...not to mention Mr Plummer and Molly. I haven't had a moment's peace." He chuckled, and Penny knew he was grateful for the servants' devotion. She didn't like to ask whether Juliet had visited after getting back from the theatre in the early hours.

Penny stood at the window for a moment, looking out. A pale winter sun was just starting to rise over the eastern horizon, turning the sky from grey to the palest blue. She could see Wilfred hobbling along on his crutches towards the barn, with the cat daintily picking her way behind him through the snow, and George was already hefting forkfuls of hay over the fence for the sturdy cob horses who went outside during the day, regardless of the weather.

"Perhaps a horse ride would be a nice way for you to spend a few hours?" Sir Henry suggested. He sat up a little higher and reached for the cup of hot chocolate that Molly had left by his bedside. "In fact, I'd like George to ride the estate boundary if it's stopped snowing to check we haven't had any poachers. Why don't you go with him? It would be a good way to start mulling over a few ideas for the new horses, don't you think?"

"I don't want to be too far away," Penny said hastily. She wondered whether he had an inkling about the special connection she felt to George but then felt a pang of guilt about Arthur, who had been attentively visiting her since the ball.

"Are you sure it's not something else that's on your mind?" Henry said. He raised his bushy eyebrows and gave her an enquiring look.

Penny wondered whether she could confide in him and then decided she had nothing to lose. "When I was growing up at Maude's in Sketty Lane, George was my best friend."

Henry nodded. "That's good. He seems like a fine young man."

"I…I think if I hadn't come here, we might have ended up courting," she said hesitantly. "I tried to put him from my mind over the last few years, and Arthur Sinclair…Benedicts's cousin was very kind to me at the ball. He's visited me to take tea several times since then as well."

"I sense some sort of *but* coming…" Henry's gaze was shrewd. "Is that correct?"

"Well…yes, I suppose so. It's all very confusing," Penny continued with a worried frown. "Since George came to work here instead of Melbury House, I enjoy his company." She twisted her handkerchief and sighed. "George is very polite, Grandpapa, and I know he respects the fact that my position in society is very different now from when I lived at Maude's, so he would never behave inappropriately."

"Well, I'm sure Arthur Sinclair would make an excellent match for you, Penny if that's what is troubling you. It's a shame you don't have your mama to help you with matters of the heart, but all I can say is that a man of his standing would be more than suitable for you." He gave her another shrewd look. "The thing is…do you like Arthur?"

Penny sighed again and then brightened. "I don't know, Grandpapa. But it's of no consequence because what matters at the moment is getting you better."

"Well, if you wouldn't mind accompanying George on his ride today, I'd be very grateful. And then you can tell me all about it when you return."

Penny could see that Sir Henry was tiring again, so she nodded and tiptoed away. As she went to change into her riding habit, she thought about what he had just said, but her mind was still as confused as before. Without a doubt, Arthur would make a suitable husband, and he was the right social standing for a woman of her position as the granddaughter of Sir Henry. But she also recognised that part of her heart still belonged to George. The problem was she didn't know whether George felt the same way.

"How is your grandfather?" George asked as soon as he saw Penny walking towards the stables.

"His usual incorrigible self," she replied with a smile. "The servants are all taking good care of him, so he suggested I should accompany you to ride around the estate. He said we're to check for poachers, although I think that really it's so I don't spend all day worrying about him."

"He's a very wise man." George called to Wilfred, who was back on his chair sorting through a box of old horseshoes for the black-smith. "Miss Penny and I are riding out. Will you be alright here without me?"

"Of course," Wilfred scoffed. He rolled his eyes. "You don't need to namby-pamby me, George. I can get around just fine with me crutches, although the day I can throw 'em on the fire can't come soon enough."

Penny and George set off shortly afterwards at a sedate trot. The crisp winter air was refreshing after the stifling heat of Sir Henry's room, and Penny was glad that he had suggested the outing. It also made her realise what a welcome relief it was to be in George's company. His uncomplicated friendship was something she had missed, especially with the tangled web of secrets around Juliet, which she still hadn't told anyone about.

The familiar landscape appeared very different under the pillowy mounds of snow which had settled overnight. The deer looked majestic under the bare branches of the mighty oak trees in the parkland, and smoke drifted up from the workers' cottages which were dotted across the estate. The scent of woodsmoke filled Penny with a sense of nostalgia for the Christmasses she had spent in Willow Cottage with Maude and the others. Even though money had been in short supply, somehow, they had always managed to enjoy themselves.

"Is something worrying you?" George asked as they approached the furthest boundary. "You're not usually this quiet."

"I just wonder what would have happened if I'd never discovered Sir Henry was my grandfather," Penny mused. "I don't want to sound ungrateful, but Christmas with Juliet is always rather formal. She likes everything just so, and I miss the ones Maude used to do for us."

George chuckled. "You're right. What with Nell and Jacob squabbling over the last roast potatoes and Tom's singing, they were always lively. There's no reason why you can't make it fun at Talbot

Manor, though, is there? Surely Annabel and Oscar are good company?"

"Yes, they are." Penny gave him a bright smile. "Don't mind me. I'm just a bit worried about the future and what it holds if Grandpapa…" Her words trailed off as she didn't want to contemplate his death.

"Look!" George's attention was diverted as he pointed towards the woods. "There are tracks in the snow."

Sure enough, there were footsteps that marred the pristine whiteness, and Penny shivered because she knew there would be no cause for any of the workers to be over on this part of the estate. "Who do you think it might be?"

"I don't know, but we'd better follow them. There might be a simple explanation, or it could be poachers. The meat from the estate's deer would fetch a tidy sum of money if someone stole one to butcher and sell."

Penny reined her horse to turn into the woods, following behind George. After the brightness of the morning, it felt suddenly gloomy, even though the trees were well-spaced apart. She realised it was because of the slate grey clouds rolling in from the west, blotting out the winter sun, and pulled her cloak tighter.

They rode in silence for a few minutes until George circled around and came alongside Penny. Fat snowflakes had started to fall and were already beginning to conceal the tracks ahead of them. "I think it's probably just someone out trapping rabbits," he said quietly. "Some of the villagers find it hard to feed their families at this time of year."

Penny nodded. "I don't think we need to tell Grandpapa about this. We can spare a few rabbits. In fact, I think I'll suggest that we should put together some food hampers to help the needy. It's the least we can do."

A sudden rumble of thunder overhead made their horses shift uneasily beneath them, and seconds later, the snow was falling so fast it was hard to see where they had just come from.

"We need to take shelter," George called. The wind picked up, whipping the bare branches around them and making the snowflakes swirl dizzyingly. "There's a rundown cottage just up ahead." He leaned over and grabbed the reins of Penny's horse which was growing increasingly skittish, and urged his horse forward.

It was all Penny could do to hang on, and she

was grateful for the way George seemed to be able to calm her horse with nothing more than a steady hand and quiet words of reassurance.

After what felt like an age in the disorientating snow, they reached a clearing in the woods, and Penny was surprised to see the outline of a modest dwelling. Some of the slates had fallen off the roof, and there was a thicket of brambles against the far wall, but other than that, its solid stone walls were a welcome sight. She nimbly dismounted, and George led both the horses towards an old lean-to barn at one side.

"It will probably pass quite quickly," George said once he had tethered the horses securely and come into the main part of the cottage.

Penny peered out of the doorway, feeling mesmerised by the swirling snowflakes. Even though they had only been riding for about half an hour, it felt as though they were all alone, marooned in some unrecognisable landscape and separate from normal life back at the manor.

"It's beautiful, don't you think?" she said, turning to George.

"Perfect," he replied.

She blushed slightly as she noticed that he was looking at her, not the snow beyond. Their isolation created a sense of intimacy which reminded her of the time they had gone ice skating all those years ago, and he had kissed her.

"What do you think the future holds?" George asked. His tone was casual, but Penny could sense the intensity of his feelings behind them. The look in his eyes took her straight back to that moment on the frozen river again, and she found herself wishing he would kiss her just like he had before.

Penny knew she could trust George and felt the urge to confide in him. "Grandpapa spoke to me about it yesterday, as it happens." She pulled a face which made him smile.

"I know that look. Would I be right in thinking you didn't like what he said?"

Penny shrugged. "It's not that I don't like it, more that it took me by surprise. I have always assumed that Juliet would inherit Talbot Manor as she's Grandpapa's wife. With provision for me to live here, I'd hoped. But that's not what he wants."

"He's not casting you out, is he?" George sounded indignant. He stepped forward and took Penny into his arms, looking deep into her eyes. "I'll always look after you, Penny. No matter what happens. Like I've always said...what would I do without you?" He brushed his thumb over her cheek, and his eyes crinkled into a smile that made Penny's pulse quicken, and she could feel the heat between them. "I won't let you be turned out onto the street, and frankly, I'm shocked that Sir Henry would do such a thing." He folded his arms, looking suddenly cross.

"No, you've got it wrong; he would never do that, George. You know he's kindhearted." Penny paced back and forth with a frown on her face before blurting out what was causing her so much confusion. "He told me that I will inherit Talbot Manor, George. He wants to make up for how he wronged Mama in the past, forbidding her from being with Jack, which made her run away." She shook her head in disbelief as she looked out at the woods and land beyond. "How would I manage to look after a place like this on my own?"

George's expression was hard to read as he stepped back slightly. "You underestimate yourself, Penny. Sir Henry is an astute businessman, and he is very fond of Talbot Manor. He wouldn't have left it to you if he didn't think you were capable of taking it on. It's a gesture of how much he believes in you."

"But what about Juliet?" Penny said, looking even more worried. "She will never accept me as head of the household. I'm sure she will be furious when the time comes, and she finds out."

George gave her a sympathetic look. "You're a Calder, Penny, and being mistress of Talbot Manor and looking after Sir Henry's fortune is your destiny. It's time to leave behind that raggedy little girl of the past who lugged bricks for a living, doing Mr Culpepper's bidding. Juliet will just have to come to terms with it."

"I'm not so sure," Penny sighed. She peered out of the door again to see that the snowstorm had been shortlived, just as George had predicted. "We should ride back now," she said with a hint of regret in her voice. "I don't want to leave Grand-papa too long."

As they trotted back towards the imposing manor house a while later, Penny glanced surreptitiously at George's rugged profile. She had been so sure that he might kiss her again, but now the moment had passed. Although he had offered to look after her, she couldn't tell if it had merely been out of kindness or whether it meant more. He hadn't said he loved her, and now it seemed she might never know.

Next to her, George's thoughts were in turmoil. The news Penny had just told him changed everything. She could never marry a man like him...a lowly coachman, not even now that he was taking on more responsibility, and he would never compromise her by making her choose. He thought about Arthur Sinclair, who he had seen paying several visits in recent weeks. He was good-looking, wealthy and well-connected. The perfect social match for Penny, of course. Although George wanted nothing more than to sweep Penny into his arms and had long hoped that fate would somehow allow them to spend their lives together, he now knew that it could never be. Worse still, he would have to stay silent because it wouldn't be right to do anything to jeopardise the future that Sir Henry wanted for Penny...the future that she deserved.

CHAPTER 17

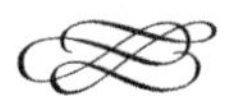

An air of worry hung over the household during the following days, seeping into every nook and cranny of the manor like a pall of smoke. Sir Henry's health was declining fast, and Doctor Grant was unable to provide even a sliver of hope that his situation would improve in spite of Penny's fervent prayers that it might.

Molly and the other maids tiptoed around, speaking in muted voices, and Mrs Pratt's face was set in a permanently mournful expression. Even Mr Plummer's usually neutral features looked downcast as he hobbled along the corridors.

Everyone was expecting the worst, but Juliet was finding the gloom almost intolerable.

"What are your plans for tomorrow?" she asked

Annabel brightly over dinner one evening. "Is Benedict visiting to take tea? Goodness knows we could do with some company. The house is starting to feel like a mausoleum, the way the servants are creeping around."

"He thought you would prefer not to have visitors at the moment," Annabel replied. "Sir Peregrine and Benedict know this is a difficult time for us."

"Life must carry on as normal," Juliet declared. "The last thing we want is for Benedict to think that you're no longer courting, Annabel. He's a good catch, and there are plenty of young ladies who would willingly take your place in his affections." She sipped her after-dinner cup of coffee at the same time as giving her daughter a firm look.

"I'm inclined to agree," Penny said.

Annabel and Oscar both looked surprised.

"Grandpapa wouldn't want everyone moping around. He has said to me many times that he's led a happy life with more good fortune than many could ever imagine. I think he would want us to get on with things as normally as possible."

Juliet gave Penny a gracious nod. It wasn't often that they agreed on something. "You must send a note to Benedict that he may visit tomorrow as planned, Annabel. And Oscar...perhaps Miss Appleby would like to visit as well when she's next down from London."

"What about Christmas?" Annabel pondered. Her expression had brightened at the thought of seeing Benedict again, and Penny wondered whether he might ask for her hand in marriage over the festive season. "Would it be inappropriate if we have a Christmas tree and do the usual decorations?"

"Certainly not. You know Christmas is Grandpapa's favourite time of year. He loves to see Talbot Manor looking festive."

"You can arrange all of that," Juliet said airily to Penny. "Tell George to choose a tree from the woods and make sure it's a good one. We don't want visitors to feel as though standards are slipping just because Henry is ill."

Penny poured herself a cup of coffee, hoping that nobody would notice the flush of heat on her cheeks at the mention of George's name. The memory of his strong arms around her in the abandoned cottage was still fresh in her mind, and her heart skipped a beat as she thought about the way his brown eyes had been full of concern for her.

"I was thinking it would be a nice gesture to make up some food parcels for the villagers and estate workers." Penny sipped her coffee.

"Food parcels?" Juliet frowned as she echoed Penny's words. "The farm workers are paid more than enough to buy their own food, and what the villagers do is none of our concern. Edmund says that most of them are idle layabouts anyway."

"I don't agree with that," Oscar replied sharply. "Besides, it's nothing to do with Edmund, Mama. I think it's a good idea of Penny's, especially as it has been so cold this winter. The snow came earlier than usual, so root vegetables are in short supply, and some of them are struggling to feed their families."

"I'm not sure I like your tone, Oscar," Juliet said with a pout. "You shouldn't be so dismissive of Edmund's opinion. He has all sorts of plans for Talbot Manor should the time come when I need his advice. And it certainly won't involve throwing good money after bad on the lazy villagers. Henry wanted to give all the workers a few extra coins for Christmas, but I put a stop to it because they'll only waste it on ale."

Oscar looked shocked. "That's not a kind way to look after our servants and neighbours, Mama.

We have so much, and you won't even spare them a little bit of extra money for some Christmas cheer. If that's what Edmund thinks, then he's a very bad influence."

Juliet glared mutinously at Penny and then at Oscar. "Fine…do as you like. I find it all rather tedious anyway." She stood up and dabbed a napkin daintily on her lips, glancing at Molly. "Don't just stand there; clear the table. And then stoke the fire in my parlour."

"Yes, m'lady." Molly scurried forward and started rattling the dishes as she gathered them up, which made Juliet wince with irritation.

"Edmund is taking me shopping and out for luncheon tomorrow," she said, giving Penny a defiant look. "All this business with Henry's lingering ill health is very upsetting for me, and Edmund said a day out will do me the world of good."

"It's upsetting for everyone," Penny muttered. It seemed that Juliet's friendship with Edmund knew no bounds, and she felt a surge of resentment that tongues were probably already wagging about how much time Edmund was spending with Juliet while her poor Grandpapa was being made to look a fool.

. . .

A LITTLE WHILE LATER, Penny crept into Sir Henry's bedroom. His breathing was laboured, and the quietness of the room made each breath sound as though it was a huge effort to drag into his congested lungs. "How are you, Grandpapa?" She pressed a cool compress on his forehead, which Doctor Grant had said might help him feel more comfortable. The water in the bowl smelt of Mrs Pratt's lavender oil, and Molly had put pine cones on the fire to release their resinous scent in an attempt to cheer the master up.

Henry's eyes fluttered open, and it took him a moment to focus on Penny. Once he saw it was her, he smiled. "Don't feel bad for me, dear girl. I have made my peace with the inevitable." His voice was little more than a whisper, and Penny had to bend over to hear him.

"It's not long until Christmas, Grandpapa," she said, trying to keep her voice cheerful. "George is going to cut down a lovely fir tree from the woods, and we'll decorate the entrance hall, as long as you don't mind?"

"I wouldn't have it any other way," he replied croakily. "And even if I'm no longer here, you must always celebrate Christmas, Penny...and use the opportunity to spread a little bit of joy to others as well."

"Oscar and I are going to deliver food parcels to the villagers," Penny told him, pleased to be rewarded with another smile.

"That's why you will inherit...it's what I want..."

Penny leaned closer. Her grandfather's voice was getting weaker, and she felt a sense of regret in the pit of her stomach that there was nothing more she could do for him. His eyes closed, and she straightened the coverlet, thinking that he had drifted off to sleep again. She stoked the fire and turned to leave, but just as she reached the door, his eyes opened again.

"Penny? There's something else...it's been on my mind..." This time there was a note of urgency in his voice.

"What is it, Grandpapa? Is there something I can get for you?" She hurried back to his bedside.

"When I told Louisa she couldn't see...Jack..." His brow furrowed with the effort of speaking. "Don't make the same mistake...follow...follow your heart, Penny..."

Penny blinked back sudden tears at how frail

her grandfather looked. His wispy white hair was like a halo around his head, and the blue veins stood out on the backs of his hands. Yet, even though she knew he didn't have much longer, she was touched that he was thinking of how he could help her.

"I'm not sure what my heart is telling me yet, Grandpapa," she said softly. "But when I know, I promise I will keep your words in mind."

Henry gave her a faint smile and then lifted his hand feebly to wave her away. "Leave me to rest now, my dear. I'll see you again in the morning."

Penny tossed and turned in her bed after reading a book for a little while to try and take her mind off things. She still hadn't had a chance to talk to her grandfather more about the inheritance and didn't even know whether he had told Juliet of his plans. Added to that, her confusion over George and Arthur was making sleep even more elusive. Eventually, the slow, even breathing of Bramble at the foot of her bed lulled Penny into a fitful doze, and finally, she drifted into a deep, dreamless sleep.

A sudden shriek split the air, and Bramble

hurled himself at the door, letting off a volley of deep barks.

"What is it?" Penny's heart hammered in her chest, and she lifted her night candle with trembling hands as another bloodcurdling scream reached her ears. She hastily tied her lace-trimmed velvet dressing gown over her nightgown and hurried out onto the landing.

"Miss Penny, come quickly!" Molly's voice floated up the stairs, and Penny saw her pale upturned face below her. "We've been burgled."

Doors started slamming as various servants came running to see what the commotion was, and Bramble's hackles were up as he stuck to Penny's side.

"What the devil's going on?" Oscar came running towards her, and they both hurried downstairs.

"I went into Sir Henry's study to add some wood to the fire," Molly explained, glancing nervously over her shoulder at the shadowy corners of the hallway. "He asked me not to let the room get damp from the cold...and I hoped that he might be able to come down to his study again soon when he gets better."

"Thank you, Molly, that's very thoughtful."

Penny patted her shoulder, trying to calm the poor girl down. "And then what happened?"

"Well, I went into the study, and the window was wide open, Miss Penny." Her eyes filled with tears, and she looked at Oscar. "I promise it weren't me, sir. I would never leave the window open in this weather, even though Lady Calder tells me I'm a scatterbrain."

Oscar seized a walking stick from beneath the coat rack and held it aloft. "I will go and check that the intruder has left. You stay here."

"Wait. Bramble and I will come with you," Penny said. She grabbed the lamp out of Mr Plummer's hands, and they hurried down the dark corridor. The lamp swung in Penny's hands, making tall shadows loom over them, but she wasn't afraid. If anything, she felt indignant that someone would do such a thing when Sir Henry was so ill.

"These rooms all look untouched," Oscar said, quickly opening the doors they passed to check if they were alright.

Penny gasped as they entered the study. It had been ransacked, and there were books and papers strewn all over the floor. The drawers of Sir Henry's desk were still open, and the curtains flapped in the icy breeze which was blowing through the window. Bramble growled and darted into every corner of the room, nose down, sniffing the floor, before running to the window and whining.

"Whoever did this is long gone," Oscar said. He slid the heavy sash window closed as Penny surveyed the mess.

"Why would they come into Grandpapa's study? He only keeps books and his work documents in here." She quickly lit several other lamps and had a better look around. The cut glass decanter he kept on the side with brandy in it was still there, as was the silver cigar box.

"All I can think is that Molly disturbed them. You know how she likes to sing as she's going about her duties. The person probably heard her coming and left before they had a chance to take anything of value." Oscar checked in every corner and gave her a rueful smile. "For once, Molly's noisiness might have served us well. I think we all need a cup of hot chocolate to calm our nerves."

Penny nodded. "Good idea; I'll ask Daphne to warm some milk for us. Molly might even need a nip of brandy in hers, otherwise, she'll never sleep after getting such a fright."

Before Penny had a chance to speak to the cook to make them all a hot drink, Annabel came running down the stairs with the ribbons of her ruched nightgown flying out behind her. "What's happening?" she cried.

"We've been burgled," Molly said, breaking into a fresh bout of tears as she trembled next to Mr Plummer. "Someone's been in Sir Henry's study and turned it upside down…I ain't ever seen the like of it."

"You mean they've been in the house while we were all here?" Annabel's voice rose to a panicked shriek. "Oscar, do something…send George to fetch the constable…"

Penny saw a movement at the top of the stairs. "Grandpapa. What are you doing out of bed?"

"I heard a commotion," he replied. "Is anyone going to tell me what this is all about?" He swayed, still looking half asleep, and Penny started to run up the stairs towards him.

"We've been robbed," Annabel sobbed. "Some terrible person has come in the dead of night. We're not even safe in our beds."

Sir Henry's suddenly clutched at his chest and fell to the floor with a sickening thud.

"Lord preserve us...the master's had a seizure," Mrs Pratt said in a horror-stricken tone.

Tears pooled in Penny's eyes as she knelt next to Sir Henry. "Fetch Doctor Grant," she cried. But as she touched her grandfather's lifeless hand, she already knew it was too late.

CHAPTER 18

"To the left a bit, George." Molly cried excitedly. Her eyes were shining as she stood back on the far side of the entrance hall and called out her instructions.

"Are you sure? We don't want it too close to the fire in case it gets hot and drops all the needles."

"We ain't never had a tree this big before. Mr Webster always said Abigail thought it was ostentatious to have something so grand, but I like the one you've chosen."

"What about here?" George's voice was muffled as he struggled to manoeuvre the prickly fir tree to the best position.

"That's perfect," Penny said, making Molly jump guiltily.

"Sorry, Miss Penny. I didn't mean to sound so happy, what with us all still being in mourning." She looked down at the scuffed toes of her boots and sniffed as tears suddenly filled her eyes. "If I'd never told anyone about the burglary, Sir Henry would still be alive...it's all my fault," she wailed.

"Now then, Molly, what have I told you?" Penny pulled a lace handkerchief from her pocket and handed it to the forlorn maid, giving her a kind smile. "Doctor Grant said Sir Henry was lucky to have lasted for so long, given how bad his lungs were. And in many ways, the seizure was a blessing in disguise. It meant that his death was quick, and he wasn't in any pain."

"Are you sure, Miss Penny?" Molly blew her nose noisily and dragged her sleeve across her eyes to dry her tears. "My nerves are in tatters...one minute, I feel happy about it nearly being Christmas, and then, the next, I remember he's not with us anymore." Her chin trembled, and Penny squeezed her shoulder to reassure her.

"It's a strange time for all of us, but we have to carry on. It's what Grandpapa would have wanted, and he was very fond of you, Molly. He always said you brightened his day."

"Cheer up, Molly," George chimed in. "Sir

Henry loved Christmas, so we shall make it the best one yet, in his memory."

Penny and George exchanged a knowing smile as Molly started singing a carol a moment later as she set about dusting the picture frames.

"Are you sure you're up to this?" George asked Penny quietly. "It's only been two weeks since the funeral, and you must miss him." The concern in his eyes was almost her undoing, and she took a shaky breath before nodding.

"Keeping busy is very helpful. Speaking of which, will you drive the cart for me when I deliver the food parcels around the village? Some of them might feel a bit shy about accepting our charity as this is the first year we've done it, so it will be nice for them to see it's not just the Calder family members bestowing gifts."

"I have the common touch, is that what you mean?" George asked with a good-natured chuckle. When Penny nodded, he laughed again. "You do as well if you did but realise it, Penny. Most of them know that you were raised by Maude, and for someone of your wealth, you don't have airs and graces like Juliet."

"I'll take that as a compliment." They worked side-by-side for a few moments in companionable silence, fastening candles to the spiky branches of the tree. Whenever she was in Arthur's company, she always felt as though she should be making witty conversation, but George was perfectly happy to leave her to her thoughts, which she was grateful for.

"I brought the box of decorations from the attic storeroom, Miss Penny."

"And these are the garlands of dried fruit that Molly and I made."

Mrs Pratt and Daphne both looked as excited as Molly had been as they gazed at the tree, which told Penny that they were doing the right thing by celebrating Christmas as usual.

"Look what we found at the back of the cupboard. I thought it was lost." Mrs Pratt held up a silver star that was exotically carved to reflect the twinkling light of the candles. "I haven't seen it for years. It was your ma's favourite because Sir Henry brought it back from one of his overseas trips when she was a little girl, and he used to hold the ladder so she could put it at the top of the tree."

"I'm not too late to join in, am I?" A dragging sound announced Mr Plummer's arrival, and he hobbled towards them, pulling a wooden stepladder behind him.

"Let me help with that." George sprang forward and took it off him, positioning it next to the tree.

"The star is a bit battered, but maybe you'd like to follow tradition and put it on the tree?" Mrs Pratt handed the ornament to Penny, looking misty-eyed with emotion.

Penny climbed slowly up the rungs of the ladder and carefully put the star in position. Her heart swelled with the significance of the occasion as she thought about her mother doing it before her, with her grandpapa's help.

"Be careful coming down again," Daphne said, brushing away tears of happiness at the sight of the old silver star in its rightful place again. "We don't want any accidents."

"I've got the ladder, you're quite safe." George's arms encircled Penny momentarily as she reached the bottom rung again, and she felt a dart of pure joy that he was sharing this special time with her. He smiled as their eyes met, and suddenly all of Penny's confusion melted away. Sir Henry had advised her to follow her heart, and now she knew with absolute certainty what she had to do.

. . .

"ARE WE EXPECTING VISITORS?" Molly interrupted the moment and hurried to the front door to look outside as the clopping of horses and the crunch of carriage wheels on the sweep grew louder. "It's Sir Henry's brother," she added, looking to Penny for guidance.

"I thought we weren't receiving guests at the moment?" Mrs Pratt muttered under her breath with a disapproving sniff. "The master's barely been buried two weeks."

"Mr Calder is here at my request," Juliet said airily as she glided into the hallway. "Please prepare tea and coffee for everyone, Mrs Fraser. I want the family to gather in the drawing room in half an hour once Mr Calder and I have had a chance to speak privately about a few matters. He's here about Sir Henry's will."

Penny couldn't help but notice that Edmund seemed in good spirits as he breezed into the house and thrust his hat and coat at Mr Plummer.

"Good morning, everyone," he boomed. "Fetch one of Henry's finest bottles of brandy from the cellar, will you please, Mrs Pratt. It's so cold out today that I could do with a nip of something." He linked arms with Juliet, and they vanished into her parlour, leaving Mrs Pratt open-mouthed with shock at his display of over-familiarity.

"Well, I'll be..." she said huffily. "Sir Henry's best brandy, is it?" She flounced off, and Daphne and Molly hurried after her. The festive mood from decorating the tree had fizzled out, and they knew better than to keep Lady Calder waiting.

"Did you know he was coming today?" George asked Penny.

Penny shook her head. "I can only assume he's here to actually read the will," she replied. "He was Grandpapa's solicitor, although I think it's just a formality since Grandpapa said he left Talbot Manor to me." She looked suddenly nervous. "If that is what he's going to do, would you sit in with us, George? You're an important part of the estate, with the horse breeding project that he wanted you to undertake. I'm sure the others won't mind."

"I'm not sure that Lady Calder would agree." George had been on the receiving end of Juliet's sharp tongue on more than one occasion and knew that, unlike Penny, she was a stickler for the servants knowing their place. "I'll wait out here in the hallway instead," he suggested. "It looks like you need more logs fetching for all the fires, so I can do that and won't be far away if you need me to get involved."

ANNABEL STIFLED a yawn as they all gathered around the blazing fire in the drawing room a little while later. Her mind was distracted thinking about all the heavy hints that Benedict had been dropping about them getting engaged before Christmas, and she had barely slept out of excitement the night before.

"Will this take long, Edmund?" Oscar pulled off his gloves as he came in, still in his riding boots. "There are problems with the animals because of the water freezing, and I promised the farm workers I would help them sort it out."

"You shouldn't be out in the cold doing the work for them," Juliet said, looking annoyed.

"It's not for them, Mama; it's with them." Oscar shrugged and picked up one of the cups of coffee that Molly had poured. He knew he would never get his mother to understand that the workers appreciated his approach of being willing to muck in when needed, so there was no point trying.

Edmund tipped a generous splash of brandy into his cup of coffee and took a mouthful of it before going to stand in front of the fire. With his legs apart and hands behind his back, gazing at them all, he looked every inch as though he owned the place, Penny thought.

"It's won't take very long at all, Oscar. You can be back out in the mud and snow again in no time," Edmund said, exchanging an amused look with Juliet, who gave him a coy smile.

He rocked forward on his feet and pulled a document out of the inner pocket of his coat.

"You all know that I am a solicitor and therefore used to dealing with legal matters, but what you might not have realised is that my dear brother, Sir Henry, entrusted me with writing his will." Edmund cleared his throat and blinked as though suddenly overcome with emotion, which surprised Penny. He hadn't looked upset during the funeral, although she supposed he could have been putting on a brave face.

Juliet leaned forward in her chair slightly, giving him her full attention. "Carry on, Edmund. I know this is a difficult time for all of us, but we can't leave things hanging."

"Quite." Edmund unfolded the document with an air of self-importance. "It's a short will and simple in its contents, which is what Henry wanted."

Penny took a sip of tea. Her hands were trembling as she braced herself for Juliet's disappointment if the outcome was going to be a surprise.

"I'm not sure this really concerns me," Annabel blurted out as the tension mounted. "I didn't want to say anything yet because of being in mourning, but Benedict has as good as asked me to become his wife, so I will be living at Blaenwen Hall after the wedding."

Edmund rustled the document again, looking annoyed that Annabel had interrupted him. "That's wonderful news, Annabel. Your mama said an engagement was likely...but can we get back to the matter at hand?"

Penny reached across and gave Annabel's hand a surreptitious squeeze, wanting to show that she was happy for her, and Annabel shot her a grateful smile.

"So what does it say?" Oscar asked, glancing at the grandfather clock in the corner of the room.

Edmund cleared his throat again, making sure that everyone was paying attention. "Sir Henry has instructed that Juliet is to inherit Talbot Manor in its entirety, plus all his business assets." He looked at them all and then gave Juliet a beaming smile. "That's not all," he continued. "Juliet and I have some other news…we're to be married. In all likelihood, we shall sell this draughty old pile as soon as possible and move to London."

What?" Annabel looked horrified.

"Married? But…Sir Henry has only just died." Oscar's face darkened as he glared at Edmund.

"This can't be right," Penny felt her head starting to spin. "Grandpapa told me several times that his will said Talbot Manor was coming to me…with provision for you all to live here as well, of course." She jumped up, unable to sit still a moment longer. "He was adamant that he wants me to continue all the good work he has done… with Oscar managing the estate and George breeding horses…"

"You must have been mistaken," Edmund said smoothly.

"Sir Henry barely knew what day of the week it was when he was ill," Juliet snapped. "Why on earth would he leave everything to you, Penny? It's only right that he put me first. Let's not forget that you were just a labourer at Culpepper Bricks a few short years ago, being raised by Maude Bevan." Her tone was laced with contempt, and she looked to Edmund for support, who was nodding vehemently.

"The will is very clear, Penny. Did you honestly believe that Sir Henry would leave something this valuable to a…a common girl like you?" He shook his head and chuckled as though the idea was preposterous.

"Let me see the will," Oscar said suddenly. He stood up and crossed the floor in three long strides, taking it out of Edmund's hand before he could say anything.

"Does this look right to you?" Oscar handed it to Penny with a suspicious frown on his face.

"What do you think you're doing," Edmund blustered. "I'm an experienced solicitor with a proven record of working for some of the wealthiest clients in the land, and you have the cheek to doubt what I'm saying."

"We all know you've had some shady dealings in your past," Oscar said. He folded his arms and watched as Penny tilted the document towards the window to examine it.

"I beg your pardon…you…you upstart." Edmund pushed past Oscar and gave Penny a triumphant smile, jabbing his finger at the paper.

"Look, it's all there, just as I said. And signed by Sir Henry."

"This is not Grandpapa's signature," Penny replied slowly, giving Edmund a shrewd look.

"Of course it is," Juliet cried. "I think the grief has addled your mind, Penny. You're being very rude indeed, and I won't tolerate it." She hurried to Edmund's side and slipped her hand into the crook of his arm. "I've put up with you out of the goodness of my heart all these years, but now that I'm sole heir and Lady of Talbot Manor, I insist that you must leave."

"Did you ever even love Grandpapa?" Penny shot back.

"What a ridiculous question." Juliet's lips were pinched with annoyance. "Give me the will, and go and pack your bags."

"Wait." Annabel threw her hands into the air. "None of this is making any sense. Why do you say it's not Sir Henry's signature, Penny?"

"This part here is all wrong," Penny said firmly, pointing at the swirl of black ink at the end of the signature. "I've watched Grandpapa sign dozens of letters over the years, and I know this is not his writing. It must be a forgery."

"I say…this is an outrageous accusation,"

Edmund roared. His face had turned red with agitation, and he lunged to try and grab the document back off her, but Oscar blocked his way.

"Why don't you go and fetch one of Sir Henry's letters, Penny," Oscar said calmly. "This can all be sorted out in no time without any need for things to get nasty."

Penny nodded and hurried away, practically crashing into Molly, who was hovering outside the door with a startled expression at what she had just overheard. "What can I do to help, Miss Penny?" she whispered. "It ain't right that Mr Calder might get his hands on the place by marrying Lady Juliet and then sell your home without a second thought."

"Tell George to come to Grandpapa's study. I don't believe that Grandpapa was lying about my inheritance, so I need to try and find something which will solve this once and for all."

"Is it true? Molly said that Edmund is claiming the will leaves everything to Juliet?" George looked worried as he strode into Sir Henry's study.

"Yes, but I don't believe it's a legitimate document." Penny sighed as she put her hands on her hips and looked around the familiar room for inspiration. "I need something signed by Grandpapa, but the most recent letters before he died have all been sent."

"Is there something else you could use instead?" George rifled through the papers on the desk, knowing that Penny wouldn't mind. "Are you sure about the signature?"

"Once I was helping Grandpapa with his paperwork, and I noticed that his signature looked like part of the family crest. It's quite distinctive, and the one on the will doesn't have it. I can hardly believe that Edmund would try to defraud his own family in this way."

"But everyone knows he's long been jealous of Sir Henry's success," George replied. "It's common knowledge amongst the servants…not to mention how much time he's been spending with Juliet. Perhaps they planned this together?"

The room held so many memories for Penny that it was almost as if her grandfather had just stepped outside and would return any minute. She paused for a moment, imagining his twinkling eyes as he told her a story about the past. "Wait! I've got it. Grandpapa showed me a secret compartment in his bookcase once," she said. She hurried across the room and ran her fingers along the underside of the shelf as she had seen him do, feeling for some sort of catch, and suddenly the section sprang open just like it had before.

"He had this box specially made with Mama's embroidery on the lid. It was to keep things of sentimental value from my mama and grandmama without Juliet knowing about them."

George knelt down next to her and watched as she opened the box. "I'm not sure how this will help?"

"I remember seeing a thick vellum document at the bottom, but he never told me what it was." Penny carefully removed the locket and other trinkets before retrieving the document that lay at the bottom. "It doesn't matter what it is, as long as it has his signature on it."

"But look, it's a will," George said excitedly, pointing at the title. *Sir Henry Calder, Last Will And Testament.* His face darkened as a shocking thought occurred to him. "Do you think this is what the burglar was looking for when Sir Henry's office was ransacked? Perhaps it was even Edmund who did it?"

Penny cracked the wax seal and unfolded the paper. Tears pooled in her eyes as she read it. "It is

Grandpapa's proper will," she whispered. "He must have used a different solicitor to draw it up...I think he knew all along that Juliet and Edmund might try something like this. It was Edmund who knew her first, you see."

"We need to show this to everyone," George said. "But this time, I'm coming with you. I won't let Edmund bully you out of your inheritance."

Penny shot him a smile of gratitude as she looked around the room, sensing her grandfather's presence like a distant echo. "There's so much family history here, George. I couldn't bear it if Edmund just sold the place as if all of Grandpapa's hard work was meaningless. Not when we have so much still to achieve."

George put his arm around Penny's shoulder as they left the study. "Whatever happens, I want you to know that I'll always be happy to work for you."

"I know, George," Penny said happily. "You always were my best friend, and you still are."

As they walked through the entrance hall back towards the drawing room, Penny was surprised to see that another cart had just arrived on the carriage sweep, pulled by a thick-coated piebald cob. There was something familiar about the cart, and she paused to see who it was.

Plummer swung the door open just as she was about to tell him to ask the visitors to wait, but then Penny's surprise turned to astonishment.

"Neville? And Maude? What are you doing here? I didn't know you were friends."

Maude came puffing up the steps with Neville close behind. He took his threadbare cap off and twisted it nervously in his hands while Plummer eyed him suspiciously.

"Lawks, Penny. You won't believe what's happened." Maude fanned her face with the corner of her apron as she tried to catch her breath. "The rumours are flying about Sketty Lane faster than you could credit, and Neville was the only person I could persuade to bring me up here and tell you."

"Rumours of what?" George asked.

"Folk reckon that Edmund Calder is now the owner of Culpepper Bricks, and he's selling the place off," Maude cried indignantly. "Mr Culpepper's out of a job, and we're all being thrown out of our houses onto the street…right before Christmas, too."

"Maude's right, Miss Calder," Neville said darkly. "The whole town is buzzing with gossip about it…typical toff, thinking he can do what he likes without a thought for hardworking families."

Penny turned to George, and her brown eyes glittered with anger. "I won't let him get away with this. Mr Plummer, kindly take our guests to the kitchen for a cup of tea, and leave me to deal with Edmund Calder."

She tossed her head and marched towards the drawing room, clutching the precious document tightly to her chest.

"THIS IS my grandpapa's Last Will and Testament, Edmund, the proper one," Penny said a moment later, holding it up. "Would you like me to send for the constable and have you thrown into jail for committing fraud, or are you ready to accept that Grandpapa wanted me to inherit Talbot Manor?"

"The constable? Fraud?" Edmund repeated, looking nervously towards the door. His bluff and bluster had vanished to be replaced with a grovelling expression. "I'm sure this was all just a misunderstanding, Penny. Let's not do anything rash."

"We know it was you who broke into Grandpapa's study the other night," Penny shot back. The way Edmund's face paled told her that George's guess was correct. "No doubt looking for this so you could destroy it. You knew that Grandpapa wanted to leave everything to me, so you concocted a false will, thinking you could bully and lie your way into getting what you wanted."

"Is this right, Mama?" Oscar demanded.

"What will Benedict think when he finds out," Annabel said faintly.

Juliet pursed her lips and then threw her hands up in weary resignation. "Oh, alright," she said crossly. "Have it your own way, Penny. I don't even want to stay in this old manor house anyway." She had the grace to look slightly apologetic as she went to stand by Edmund's side. "Henry was very kind, but I think we all know that it was a marriage of convenience for me. My heart belonged to someone else, but I needed to marry well for Annabel and Oscar's sake."

Edmund's cheeks turned pink, and he patted Juliet's hand.

"That doesn't justify trying to rob Penny of what's rightfully hers," Annabel said, looking indignant. "Sir Henry was always very good to me."

"And me," Oscar agreed. "I suppose that means I'll have to look for work elsewhere," he added gloomily.

Penny held up her hands to stop everyone from talking. "Do you agree to give up on this false claim on Grandpapa's home and businesses?" she asked, giving Edmund and Juliet a hard stare.

They glanced at each other, and Edmund reluctantly nodded. "As long as you don't involve the law. I have my reputation with my clients to consider, and I'll need to make a decent income to keep Juliet in the manner in which she deserves."

"And what about selling off Culpepper's Brickworks and throwing all the workers out of their homes?" Penny added. She folded her arms, and Edmund shifted guiltily under her gaze.

"I...I can put the buyer off," he stuttered. "Nothing is agreed formally...I was perhaps being a little premature in claiming that it was mine to sell."

"That's all settled then," Penny replied. She took the false will from Oscar's hands and walked over to the fire, throwing it onto the flames. "Oscar and Annabel...Grandpapa was adamant that you should always be able to call Talbot Manor home." She smiled at Oscar. "You're doing such a wonderful job with the estate that I'd like you to stay if that's what you want."

Oscar nodded with relief and pulled his gloves back on again. "In that case, I'm going outside to get on with things."

"Can we please make sure that Benedict doesn't find out about all this," Annabel pleaded. "At least, not until after we're married."

"I don't see why not," Penny replied, giving her a grin. "Why don't you invite him over for our traditional Christmas eve meal? Perhaps a few glasses of Daphne's sloe gin will persuade him to confirm the engagement."

"I think I would like to stay in Melbury House for the time being," Juliet said stiffly. "Edmund and I will be married quietly sometime in the new year, but I'll understand if you don't want to come."

Penny shrugged. "I can't say yet, Juliet. You were willing to go along with Edmund's deception, or maybe it was your idea? Grandpapa didn't deserve that. For now, I have to make sure that Maude and the other people who have loyally worked for the family businesses all these years know that they're not going to be made homeless."

"I was just following my heart," Juliet replied fretfully. "I can't help the fact that I love Edmund."

"I suppose not." Penny's face was thoughtful as she walked away.

CHAPTER 19

George picked up the reins and clicked his teeth. "Gidd'up," he called to the pair of horses in front of the cart.

"Are you sure we've done enough parcels?" Penny asked. She twisted around on the seat to look behind.

"Stop worrying," George chuckled. "Molly and Wilfred have counted them at least three times, and I'm fairly sure Daphne added extra for good measure."

The winter air was crisp as the cart rumbled along the track to the first of the workers' cottages on the estate, and the low sun made the snow sparkle. Icicles hung off the bare branches of the trees, so they looked like crystal chandeliers, and their breath plumed over their heads.

"How have Annabel and Oscar taken Juliet's departure to Melbury House?" George asked. He had driven Lady Calder there in their finest carriage several days earlier, straight after the revelations about Edmund's deception, but she had studiously avoided his gaze when they arrived, choosing instead to scold one of the maids for dropping her hat box in the snow.

"I think they were so shocked about her and Edmund getting married in the new year, they were glad of her being down in Brynwell for a few weeks." Penny gave George a sideways glance. "I saw them in an embrace on the night of Sir Peregrine's ball, you know. But I convinced myself it was just a moment of madness."

"Perhaps they were in love all this time?"

"I think she was fond of Grandpapa in her own way," Penny murmured. "And I suppose there's some truth in what she said about not being able to help who we fall in love with. That's why Mama ran away to be with my pa, after all. Juliet isn't a bad woman; she was just misguided and got swept away with Edmund's plan to own the manor so he could sell it to make more money."

"There you go, thinking the best of people again." George lifted his hand to wave as one of the shepherds doffed his hat from the side of the lane. "I'm not sure I could be so forgiving."

"I'm just grateful that I have all of this and that Grandpapa broke with tradition to entrust it to me," Penny said, sweeping her arms wide to take in all the land and Talbot village. "I have so many plans, George. I can barely sleep at night with all the ideas of how I might be able to improve the lives of the poorest people in Brynwell."

"Well, donating Christmas treats is a good way to start." The first cottages came into view, and doors flew open as tousle-headed children came running out to greet them.

"How did they know we were coming?" Penny laughed as one of the young children ran alongside the cart and then clambered up and sat on her lap, much to the dismay of the lad's mother. "It's fine, I don't mind," Penny assured her.

"You didn't think Molly and Wilfred would keep news like this from the villagers, did you?" George pulled on the reins, and the horses came to a halt.

"Thank you, Miss Calder...you ain't got no idea what a blessing it is, you giving us extra food."

Widow Cranford leaned over her gate and grasped Penny's hands, thanking her profusely as her brood of eight children bobbed their heads and curtsied politely.

"There's no need to stand on ceremony," Penny said, feeling suddenly shy. She handed out the parcels of food, feeling a swell of happiness in her chest at being able to bring pleasure to the workers.

"We was so pleased to hear that Sir Henry has put you in charge of the estate," Bert, the blacksmith said as he ambled over. His wife waddled behind him, rotund with their fourth child, who was due to be born any day.

"That we were, Miss Calder," she said, seizing her hand and pumping it up and down. "'T'was a terrible day for the Talbot estate, losing your grandfather." She lowered her voice. "Don't take this the wrong way, but Lady Calder always looked down her nose at us, you see. Not like you. Knowing that you grew up on Sketty Lane means you understand what life is like for us."

"Well, I want you all to know that your hard work will be rewarded," Penny replied, gaining her confidence. "George and I want to hold a meeting with all the villagers in the new year, so you can tell us how we can improve things…whether it's for the estate, the village, or Brynwell town."

"What about one of them fancy swimming baths," one of the children suggested with a giggle.

"What a grand idea." Penny glanced at George, who raised his eyebrows and then nodded. "And I think a library, plus I shall be donating to the hospital and local schools."

"S'cuse me miss, have you got any humbugs?" a small girl asked, tugging on Penny's hand.

Penny knelt down. "No, but I happen to know that Daphne Fraser, our cook, made fudge last night…with enough for every child to have a poke of fudge each."

The girl's eyes brimmed with tears of happiness. "God bless you, Miss Calder," she lisped.

"THAT WAS A GREAT SUCCESS," George said a couple of hours later as they neared the stables of Talbot Manor again on their return journey.

"You helped make it a wonderful day, George. You'll have to help me do it every year," Penny blushed as she realised his gaze was lingering on her for longer than strictly necessary.

Follow your heart. Sir Henry's words came back

to her, and she smiled. "Actually, there's something I've been meaning to tell you—"

A sudden thrumming of hoofbeats behind them interrupted Penny, and a moment later, a glossy black thoroughbred horse ridden by Arthur Sinclair pulled alongside the cart.

"Good day, Penny. I hope you don't mind me calling unannounced." Arthur lifted his hat and smiled warmly at her.

"Of course not. We've just finished taking some food and gifts to the villagers. Will you come in for some mulled wine?"

"That would be a charming way to spend Christmas eve afternoon." Arthur dismounted, and Wilfred limped over to take the reins and lead his horse away.

"Thank you, Wilfred. You will both be coming to our celebratory supper tonight, won't you?" Penny asked, looking directly at George. "It was one of Grandpapa's favourite traditions for my birthday and to get the festivities off to a good start."

"Yes, miss," Wilfred replied. George's expression was hard to read as he watched Arthur tuck Penny's hand into the crook of his arm. "Do yer think he'll be the new master soon?" Wilfred whispered, pulling a slight face. "I hope he's kind-hearted if Miss Penny's going to marry him."

ARTHUR WAS as attentive as ever, chatting lightly about local matters as Molly poured coffee for them both and offered him a slice of fruit cake.

"I heard about the altercation with Edmund," he said eventually after Molly had left. "Word gets around between the servants. I'm glad you weren't swindled out of your inheritance. Sir Henry always spoke very highly of you, which is why I felt I had to see you today."

Penny's heart started beating faster. "Arthur, you've been very kind to me ever since the ball. There's something which I need to tell you."

"And there's something I need to ask you, dear Penny." Arthur stood up and took Penny's hands in his, pulling her up, so they were facing each other. He reached into his pocket.

"I…I can't." Penny stuttered.

"Can't what?" He looked puzzled for a moment, but then a new look crept over his face. One of regret. "I came to say that my father has recently taken on some new business interests in America.

He needs me to go there to manage them for a couple of years."

"America?" Penny looked confused.

"I hope you can forgive me," Arthur continued. He showed her the piece of paper he had pulled out of his pocket. It was a ticket for his departure on the ship sailing from Liverpool the following week. "I know that you might have thought my visits would lead to a marriage proposal, Penny, but I don't think it would be fair to expect you to leave all this behind."

Penny released the breath she had been holding and broke into a broad smile. "Thank you, Arthur. For being an honourable gentleman. You're right… Talbot Manor has to come first."

"So you're not angry with me?" Arthur looked relieved. "I've been trying to pluck up the courage to do this for several days. I didn't want you to think I had toyed with your affections or ruined your reputation."

"You haven't." Penny stood on her tiptoes and kissed him on the cheek. "I wish you all the best, Arthur, and who knows, you might meet a charming American lady and make your home over there. Now, if you'll excuse me, Plummer will see you out. There's something I need to do." With that, she picked up her skirts and ran out of the parlour and across the entrance hall.

"What's got into her?" Plummer muttered.

"I think I know," Mrs Pratt replied, giving him a wink. "And not before time, either."

"WHERE'S GEORGE?" Penny called as she spotted Wilfred outside the stable. "I have some wonderful news I need to share with him."

"He's just yonder in the orchard, miss. Putting some hay out for the horses."

Penny ran through the snow, her chestnut curls flying out behind her, and clambered over the gate. Sure enough, George was forking sweet hay into a mound as the horses milled around him.

"Is everything alright?" he asked as Penny ran towards him.

"I have some news," she said breathlessly.

George carefully placed the fork to one side and gave her a smile that was slightly crooked. "I'm guessing that with Arthur's visit and the way you just jumped over that gate, it must be something good. Congratulations, Penny. Annabel hinted that there might be several weddings in the spring." He paused for a moment. "Arthur's a very lucky man to call you his wife."

Penny laughed and stepped closer. "That's not my news. I came to tell you that Arthur and I are definitely not getting married. He's going to America for business, and I'd already decided that I wouldn't be able to accept his proposal anyway because my heart belongs to someone else."

"Are you sure?" George looked at her glowing cheeks and the happiness sparkling in her eyes, and this time, his smile was broad.

"I've always loved you, George. Ever since the day you picked me up off the ice and kissed me."

He placed his arms around Penny and drew her closer, looking deep into her eyes in a way that made her heart skip a beat. "Us being together would be very unconventional, and a lot of people would disapprove of you even being friends with a lowly coachman."

"There's nothing lowly about you," Penny whispered. "And as for what people say…you should know by now that I don't care a jot about that. Grandpapa told me to follow my heart just before he died…he knew I loved you, George, and gave us his blessing. I truly believe that."

"In that case…I love you too, Penny." George

glanced up at the bunch of white-berried mistletoe which was growing in the branches of the apple tree above them. "Would you do me the very great honour of becoming my wife, Penny Frost?"

Penny closed her eyes and melted into the kiss she had long imagined as their lips met. "I never wanted to marry anyone else but you," she murmured a moment later, turning her face up for another kiss.

"Well, I'll be…" Mr Plummer muttered as he went outside to brush the snow off the steps and caught sight of them in a passionate embrace.

"Sir Henry would have been so happy to know that Penny found true love," Mrs Pratt said, dabbing a handkerchief at her eyes as she came to join him.

"That he would," Plummer said, leaning on his broom. His wizened face broke into a wide smile as the sound of Molly's singing reached them, and the scent of Christmas pudding wafted over from the kitchen. "That he would," he repeated. "Merry Christmas, Mrs Pratt. I think, in spite of everything, this might turn out to be our most wonderful one yet."

EPILOGUE

Five Years Later...

Maude bustled into Penny's dressing room and raised her eyebrows as she saw Molly laying out a red velvet gown. "Are you sure that's the one she wants to wear today?"

"Yes, Mrs Bevan. She said it ain't too tight."

"I'm sure she's been overdoing it, but there's no telling her. Penny always puts herself out for others. I only hope Lady Calder appreciates the effort." Maude sniffed with a slight air of disapproval at the mention of Juliet's name and then shared a smile of understanding with Molly.

"I thought we'd agreed to let bygones be bygones," Penny said as she came through the door. "This is Juliet and Edmund's first visit to Talbot Manor for almost two years, so I want them to feel welcome."

"I can help you into your gown," Maude said, shooing Molly away.

Penny chuckled. "She's a very capable maid, Maude. You don't have to fuss over me like a mother hen. I invited you to stay so you could relax and enjoy yourself."

"That's as maybe, Penny, but what would I do with myself if I didn't have a few little jobs to fill my day? You know I can't just sit around being idle...and if Juliet makes any rude comments about you and your family, I hope you won't expect me to just bite my tongue. She might be well-to-do, but good manners don't seem to come naturally to her."

Penny hung up her dressing gown and stepped into the velvet dress before turning around so Maude could do up the buttons. She hoped it hadn't been a mistake to invite Juliet to their New Year's Day luncheon with Maude staying as well. She knew both women could be opinionated.

"I think living in London has mellowed Juliet. And since I gifted her and Edmund Melbury House, she doesn't feel so aggrieved about me inheriting Talbot Manor. I'm sure she will be on her best behaviour, and it will be nice to have everyone together again for the day."

"At least I can help you look after all the little 'uns," Maude replied, brightening at the prospect of having something to do.

"Annabel and Benedict are bringing their two little boys. I asked if they wanted to stay the night, but they prefer to get home to Blaenwen Hall, and it's not far to go. The boys will enjoy seeing their cousins."

"Oscar and Mary don't mind sharing Talbot Manor with you then?" Maude asked.

"No, it works well. Now that Oscar is spending more time in Parliament, he likes the fact that Mary and their children have company. It's not as if we're short of space," she added with a wry smile. "Speaking of which, are you sure I can't persuade you to move to the estate, Maude? You know you're always welcome."

Maude shook her head firmly. "I like my little cottage in Sketty Lane, you know that." She picked up the silver-backed brush and ran it through Penny's glossy curls. "I have Nell and her family just around the corner, and Tom's settling into his new job as landlord of The Saddlers Arms now that he's not at sea anymore. I reckon him and Sal might be wed before the year is out."

Penny patted Maude's hand and gave her a soft smile. "I'm so grateful that you helped raise me, Maude. I won't ever forget what you did for me and Ma."

Maude waved her words away, but her eyes misted over momentarily. "It was just what anyone would have done. Besides, you and Sir Henry have repaid my bit of kindness many times over, what with giving me the cottage and helping Nell and Tom with their businesses." She smiled at Penny in the mirror. "Dare I ask how Jacob is getting on as your new butler?"

"Mr Plummer is a very patient teacher, and the role was becoming far too much for him," Penny said, laughing, but then her face grew serious again. "I don't want Jacob to ever think I consider myself above him, Maude. Are you sure he likes the job?"

"Of course he does. After all that time at Culpepper's, he's really gone up in the world, and you know he would never think that about you, Penny. It was kind of you to give him the opportunity to make something of himself." Her eyes twinkled. "I think he's sweet on Molly, though, so we might have even have two weddings to look forward to this year."

"In that case, I shall give them one of the cottages on the estate and wish them every happiness."

The clock on the mantelpiece chimed the hour, and Penny stood up. She smoothed her dress over the swell of her belly and smiled to herself as she felt the familiar flutter of a baby's kick under her hand. "I'd better go and make sure everything is running smoothly in the kitchen. Meanwhile, I insist you put your feet up for an hour, Maude. Molly will make you a cup of tea, and you can sit by the fire in my parlour if you like until our guests arrive."

Steam billowed up from the bubbling contents of the pans on top of the range, and Penny sniffed appreciatively as she entered the kitchen.

"Mama...look what Mrs Fraser let me make." Four-year-old Lillian Calder proudly held up a tray of mince tarts, and her brown ringlets bobbed with excitement around her oval face. It was a sight which never failed to warm Penny's heart.

"She's been as good as gold, Miss Penny,"

Daphne said, lifting a tray of roast beef and potatoes out of the oven.

"Just like her grandma…never happier than when she's helping us," Mrs Pratt added, giving the little girl a fond smile.

The kitchen door suddenly flew open, letting in a blast of cold air from the outside. "The sun has come out, Lillian. Do you want to help me take hay out for the horses?" George grinned as Lillian jumped off the chair and launched herself into his arms.

"Your face is cold, Pa," she said, stroking his cheeks with her little hands. "Can Ma come with us?"

"I think we have time before everyone arrives," Penny said. She lifted Mrs Pratt's woollen shawl off the hook on the back of the door and wrapped it over her shoulders.

"You can't wear that old thing," Mrs Pratt said, looking shocked. "You're the lady of the manor, miss."

Penny's eyes sparkled with merriment. "I know, but nobody will see. Don't worry; I'll make sure we're back before Juliet arrives."

The snow creaked under their feet, and Lillian wriggled in between her parents, holding hands with both of them, as they walked out towards the orchard where the horses were nuzzling the ground, looking for grass.

"It's almost time for our annual meeting with the villagers," Penny mused. "I wonder what suggestions they will have for us this year?"

George gave his wife an admiring smile. "You never fail to surprise me," he said. "You've already helped influence some of the reformations of law with your suggestions to Oscar and Sir Peregrine to take to Parliament, not to mention improving the schools and hospitals in Brynwell."

Penny shrugged, and her cheeks turned pink at the compliment. "I'm only carrying on the work that Grandpapa already started. We owe it to those less fortunate than us to make society better for them."

Lillian clapped her hands with excitement as they got closer to the horses and ran ahead to clamber up the fence rails so she could pat them.

"That's just one of the many things I love about you," George said softly as Penny linked arms with him. "All of this could have gone to your head, but you never let it."

"I have you to thank for that," Penny replied. She reached up and brushed a kiss on his cheek. "You've come up with many of the ideas on how we can help people and improve the estate. I'm very proud of you, George, and Grandpapa would have been too."

In the distance, a carriage turned through the tall gateposts, and two black horses trotted through the snow, pulling a gleaming carriage. "There's Neville, with Juliet and Edmund."

"You're a very forgiving person," George said with a chuckle. "Neville could hardly believe his luck when you suggested he should become our coachman so I could do more work with the estate. And Alf is doing a fine job of managing Culpeppers."

"Grandpapa taught me that people deserve a second chance. Plus, I've learned that there's no point in holding a grudge," Penny replied as George picked up a pitchfork and heaved some hay over the fence. "When I discovered that it was Edmund who turned Mama away from his home in Brynwell when she asked for help because he didn't want to be associated with the scandal of his runaway niece, I have to admit, I wanted nothing more to do with him for a while."

"So what changed?" George asked curiously. "I know you will be perfectly charming to them today. You even said you were happy they were coming."

Penny smiled. "If he hadn't turned Mama away that snowy night, Maude would never have found her lying in the snow and taken her in. But it was that simple act of kindness which led to me living at Sketty Lane...and ultimately to you and me meeting and falling in love."

"So you could say that it was fate...or perhaps destiny," George said. He pulled Penny into an embrace, and they shared a secret smile before kissing.

"Is it time to go back for luncheon?" Lillian asked. She clambered back down off the fence, her cheeks rosy from the cold. Smoke drifted up from the ornate chimneys of Talbot Manor into the bright blue sky, and the low winter sun glinted off the mullioned windows. They could see Wilfred hurrying out to hold the horses as the carriage drew to a halt.

"Yes, we'd better go back, otherwise, Mrs Pratt will be trying to keep the peace between Juliet and Maude, and who knows what might happen if Molly gives everyone her generous measures of mulled wine." Penny savoured the moment of happiness with just the three of them before the busy afternoon ahead as they retraced their footsteps in the snow towards the house.

"Are you wearing your special brooch today, Mama?" Lillian asked.

"Of course, my sweet." Penny pulled her shawl aside and showed her daughter the small silver brooch with the mother-of-pearl dove pinned to her collar. "Do you want to know the story of how this brooch came to be mine…and how your papa and I ended up living here?"

"Yes, please," Lillian said, skipping in the snow between them.

A pair of collar doves billed and cooed in the bare branches of the apple tree nearby, heralding that spring was not far away. It would be a year when they would welcome another baby into their family, as well as celebrate new marriages in the household. Penny's heart swelled with joy as she glanced sideways at George, and his kind brown eyes crinkled as he smiled back at her, just like they had all those years ago when she first fell in love with him.

READ MORE

If you enjoyed The Snow Orphan's Destiny, you'll love Daisy Carter's other Victorian Romance Saga Stories:

The Pit Girl's Scandal:

Accused of something so terrible, the villagers turn against her. Will Betty ever find love and happiness? Can she clear her name, or will she always be trapped by the secrets from her past?

Betty Jones accepts that her place in life is to work alongside her family in the coal mining community of Pencastle, where the Nantglas Colliery looms darkly over the village. Toiling underground is all she's ever known, so it's futile to wish for something different.

What makes it bearable is the love of her family and snatched moments of freedom with her best friend, Dylan.

But poverty and death are ever-present in the harsh conditions they work in.

As her mother's health worsens, it falls to Betty to keep a roof over their heads and food on the table. But one terrible day, as storm clouds gather over the valley, circumstances change forever down the pit.

Just when Betty needs the support of her neighbours and friends, she is accused of a deed so terrible that everyone turns against her.

She is forced to flee and finds herself propelled into the strange new world of the theatre under the protection of an uncle she never knew she had.

But certain people at the theatre are determined to see her fail, and a brush with the law leaves her vulnerable to their devious plans.

Betty fears she will be condemned to live under the shadow of her past forever.

With her secrets about to be exposed, will she ever get a chance to prove her innocence?

When her future hangs in the balance, and with the love and happiness she yearns for at stake, will Betty have the courage to save herself and her family?

The Pit Girl's Scandal is another gripping Victorian romance saga by Daisy Carter, the popular author of The Milkmaid's Secret, The Maid's Winter Wish, and many more.

* * *

Do you love FREE BOOKS? Download Daisy's FREE book now:

The May Blossom Orphan

Clementine Morris thought life had finally dealt her a kinder hand when her aunt rescued her from the orphanage. But happiness quickly turns to fear when she realises her uncle has shocking plans for her to earn more money.

As the net draws in, a terrifying accident at the docks sparks an unlikely new friendship with kindly warehouse lad, Joe Sawbridge.

Follow Clemmie and Joe through the dangers

of the London docks, to find out whether help comes in the nick of time, in this heart-warming Victorian romance story.

Printed in Great Britain
by Amazon